PRAISE FOR

SHOW ME WHERE IT HURTS

"These stories crackle with horror energy. They hiss when you look directly at them. And you might want to wash your hands after, too." —Stephen Graham Jones, author of *My Heart is a Chainsaw* and *The Buffalo Hunter Hunter*

"A delightfully varied collection of scares based on real life, from a true lover of the horror genre." —Christi Nogle, author of *Beulah* and *The Best of Our Past, the Worst of Our Future*

"I'd compare the stories in this collection to the works of Chuck Palahniuk, with a heavy dose of Grady Hendrix, and a righteous helping of Clive Barker. Zombies and cannibalism, witches and ghosts, Bigfoot and fairies, Halloween and the mundanity of a job that grinds you into dust—there is something here for everyone. So buckle up, dig in, and follow these stories into the shadows. There is sure to be something awful waiting for you there—monstrous, full of awe, and shimmering with hope." — Richard Thomas, author of *Incarnate* and *Spontaneous Human Combustion*

SHOW ME WHERE IT HURTS

ROBERT E. STAHL

JOURNALSTONE
YOUR LINK TO ARTIST TALENT

ISBN: 978-1-68510-156-5 (trade paper)
ISBN: 978-1-68510-157-2 (ebook)
Library of Congress Catalog Number: 2025941958

First printing edition: June 27, 2025
Printed by JournalStone Publishing in the United States of America.
Cover Artwork: Don Noble
Edited by Sean Leonard
Proofreading, Cover Layout, & Interior Layout by Scarlett R. Algee
Interior image from Pixabay//youllneverknow

JournalStone Publishing
1400 North Wood Rd.
Murphysboro, IL 62966

JournalStone books may be ordered through booksellers or by
contacting:
or
JournalStone | www.journalstone.com

This collection is dedicated to all the outsiders in the world—all the losers and loners, freaks and faggots, geeks and weirdos, addicts and outcasts. Channel your pain into something useful. Believe in yourselves. Show me where it hurts.

"Damaged people are dangerous. They know they can survive."
—*Damage* by Josephine Hart

"Don't you know straight hair ain't got no curl?"
—*Pop Life* by Prince

"Just keep swimming, just keep swimming..."
—Dory in *Finding Nemo*

CONTENTS

FOREWORD

I've been working with Robert Stahl for many years now, and have become quite a fan of his writing. What this collection brings to the table, is a feast for the senses—sight, sound, smell, taste, and touch. And across that elevated palette you will get a 30-course meal that runs the gamut—sweet, sour, salty, bitter, umami. Within this banquet I'd like to point out two of my favorite flavors—horror paired with humor, and maximalism layered with great authority and detail. Let's dig in, shall we?

HORROR WITH HUMOR

For me, humor and horror is such a tricky thing to do, and it doesn't always work for me. But then I think about the work of Stephen Graham Jones (such as "Wait for Night") or Rich Larson ("Quandary Aminu vs. the Butterfly Man" coming to mind) I realize that quite a few of these tales work for me—breaking up the tension of classic horror tropes to find humor in the absurd, laughing on the outside, while crying on the inside. Such a powerful combination. At his best, Robert manages to avoid regurgitating classic monsters and cliches by injecting humor into his work, with striking results. I mean, take "Loving the Beast." What I thought might turn into something silly or expected actually shows us a Bigfoot in a new light—the curiosity and legend of the monster paired with the abuses our more base desires reflect in the worst of mankind. (Have you seen the recent social media posts about man vs. bear? Yep, that's what I'm talking about.) And it doesn't turn into Bigfoot porn either (it's a thing, honest, Google it)—it instead takes us into his world with horror and humor alike. Are we really surprised that our protagonist can't soothe the savage beast?

A setting that Robert likes to showcase in this collection is the workplace, and I can't think of a better environment in which to have things go horrible wrong, as we see how the daily grind weighs heavy on our cast of characters, desperate to make things better, more interesting, more exciting. Comes at a price, dearie, right? "Evil Inc. (or How to Succeed at Business without Really Dying)"—it's all right there in the title, yeah? And yet, mixed into the humor is horror that unfolds in great details, such as this passage, a favorite of mine:

"Some ancient and vast universe pushes its way into his brain, like a blanket the size of the world, smothering everything he knows. He struggles to break free, but it's no use. There's pressure, so much pressure, building up in his shoulder blades, finally releasing in a bright explosion of pain as the flesh yields and wings sprout from his back. He is the lion, waiting in the grass. He's on a rollercoaster, and he's letting go. Already the syrup is pouring from the jar, anointing the naked flesh of the sniveling man at his feet. It's feeding time."

Just when you let your guard down to laugh at these situations, we find ourselves in the middle of the horror, looking over our shoulder, as we try to escape it.

MAXIMALISM WITH AUTHORITY

If you're familiar with my writing over the years, you're probably aware of my desire for immersion, the maximalism I like to write in my stories and novels. I like to use all five senses, and write across body, mind, and soul—to entertain, to move you, and to challenge your intellect. Some of my favorite stories in this collection do exactly that. And often it's by using authority in the form of ritual, detail, setting, and character. Let me talk about a few examples.

In "Mumbo Jumbo," right from the jump I'm fascinated:

"The last place he thought he'd meet the Devil was in Arkansas, with its silver lakes and vigorous hills, the land itself like a blessing from God. But she smiled like a Buddhist and love took root despite the peculiar things he soon discovered. Like the dolls in her closet with pins in their eyes, and her tendency to collect spider webs, rolling them into a ball the way his grandmother kept rubber bands."

By transporting me to a place and time, this story is able to grab my attention and sell me on the idea of a devil in modern times, ending with such a great line: "'Flesh is the devil,'" he sobbed as her leathery wings enfolded him."

Similarly, "The Weeds and the Wildness Yet" might be my favorite story in this collection. And it starts with the opening paragraph:

"The irony is that his wife loves the dirt. How many times over the past forty-two years has Charlie watched her out in the garden, massaging the earth with her fingers? Mildred's tomatoes and peppers are Blue Ribbon winners come fair time, her lilies and caladiums the envy of every woman in the neighborhood. She knows every gardening trick in the book: How to control aphids with sticky tape, how to squat on an upturned bucket to avoid back pains, how to scrape her nails over a bar of soap to prevent dirt from caking underneath."

Later we are immersed in the desire, longing, and grief that has manifested in his home:

"The sofa depresses next to him, and a viscous mouth clasps down over his. He yields with his lips, opens up to the flood of moist humus surging in, warm with the process of decay and twisting with the bodies of earthworms. He opens wider as the avalanche works its way past his tonsils, into his throat, his lungs, and when his eyes flicker open, he understands finally, after all this time, what she loved about the dirt."

Across this story we are lured into the garden, the darkness, where we root for a reunion, understanding what it is to love and then lose that love, curious about how far we might go in order to bring a loved one back, right? In the end, I believe it all—I watch the horror and passion unfurl, and don't look away, no, I encourage it, no matter the results—horrifying, grotesque, and unsettling. Quite often I find myself in the middle of these stories rooting for the "monster," pushing away from the light in order to see what we might conjure in the darkness. And that's a heady place to sit, in the shadows, as a variety of entities come home to roost.

IN CONCLUSION

For my last collection of stories, *Spontaneous Human Combustion*, I got the blurb of a lifetime from Chuck Palahniuk, who compared my range and ability to Lovecraft, Bradbury, and Gaiman. It moved me, meant the world to me, that praise and acceptance by an author I so respected and enjoyed. In a similar vein I'd like to end this foreword

by making some comparisons to Robert's collection here as well—the
aforementioned Chuck Palahniuk, with a heavy dose of Grady
Hendrix, and a righteous helping of Clive Barker. Sweet, sour, salty,
bitter, umami—that sounds about right. Zombies and cannibalism,
witches and ghosts, bigfoot and fairies, Halloween and the mundanity
of a job that grinds you into dust—there is something here for
everyone. So buckle up, dig in, and follow these stories into the
shadows. There is sure to be something awful waiting for you there—
monstrous, full of awe, and shimmering with hope.

—Richard Thomas

SHOW ME WHERE IT HURTS

THE WEEDS AND THE WILDNESS YET

The irony is that his wife loves the dirt. How many times over the past forty-two years has Charlie watched her out in the garden, massaging the earth with her fingers? Mildred's tomatoes and peppers are Blue Ribbon winners come fair time; her lilies and caladiums, the envy of every woman in the neighborhood. She knows every gardening trick in the book: how to control aphids with sticky tape, how to squat on an upturned bucket to avoid back pains, how to scrape her nails over a bar of soap to prevent dirt from caking underneath.

But Charlie, he's always found dirt, well...dirty. He hates the musty smell of the stuff, that suffocating feeling on his skin.

Of course, his dislike intensifies the morning he finds her lying face down in the garden. As long as he lives, he'll never forget how the dirt behaves when he turns her over. The way it clings to the whites of her eyes. The bloody clump of mud that burps out of her nostril. The grit even manages to creep into his mouth when he's trying to breathe life back into her, calling out to God to please, bring her back, for one more moment, please.

But God doesn't work that way.

Not in real life.

At the burial, he watches family and loved ones drop handfuls of dirt onto her casket. A lump forms in his throat while he tries to imagine her in there, quiet and tranquil with her arms folded against her chest, the way she often slept at night.

How long, Charlie wonders, until the body of the woman he loves disintegrates? How many years until the rains and erosion soften the casket walls, until the wet earth surges in to claim her again? Dust to dust, like the preacher says.

The thoughts gain momentum, quickly becoming too much to bear. "Stop!" he shouts, surging forward, wrestling the bucket away from the attendant.

It's his brother Sidney who pulls him away, loads him into the back of his car, and holds him until he stops shaking.

***

Sidney stays with him the next several days, insists on keeping watch. Charlie doesn't make it difficult. He spends most of his waking hours on the sofa, watching TV.

"You're gonna take root if you don't get up and do something," Sidney says, closing the door with a casserole dish in his hands. Outside, a neighbor scurries down the sidewalk to her car.

"Wish they'd leave me alone," Charlie says.

"Careful what you wish for," Sidney says. "As for this old queen, she ain't leaving until you're better."

He does leave eventually, though, when he gets bored of leftovers, just like Charlie knows he will. "Back in thirty," Sidney says, jingling his car keys. "You okay?"

"Go," Charlie says, ushering him out, locking the door behind him.

This time, he doesn't go back to the sofa. He makes his way to the bedroom closet, fumbles around for the shoebox at the back. It's not long before he's on the edge of the bed, the barrel of a pistol lodged firmly against his soft palate. He's so focused on seeing Mildred again, he doesn't hear the front door smashing open, doesn't feel the stomp of Sidney's feet in the hallway. There's a brief struggle, but it ends with Sidney bear-hugging Charlie to the ground for the second time in as many weeks.

***

"I could use these, the way I've been tackling you lately," Sidney says. He's holding up a pair of old shoulder pads, the kind a teenager might wear for football practice. They're at a garage sale Sidney finds on the way home from therapy. It's Charlie's second week with Dr. Holman.

Charlie shrugs, knows he has it coming.

This is the last place he wants to be. He's always thought of garage sales as places where people get rid of the crap they bought at

THE WEEDS AND THE WILDNESS YET

other garage sales. But what can he do? Since his suicide attempt, he's Sidney's prisoner. His brother won't leave his side.

Anyway, he owes Sidney his life, so he says nothing, watches his brother rifle through a pile of junk on a foldaway table. Sidney picks up a gaudy sequined top, holds it up to his chest. "Does this bring out my eyes?" he asks. Charlie sighs. The one drawback to having a gay brother is he's always trying to embarrass you with it.

"What it brings out is your horrible sense of style," Charlie says. Not bad, he thinks. Why should Sidney get all the zingers?

If Sidney hears him, he doesn't let on. He's busy sorting, unfolding, exploring. Charlie takes this as a cue to pick through a few piles of his own. He finds an umbrella, remembers his old one is on the fritz. When he opens it, one of the metal rods extends out too out far and the nylon shell flops open, a mess. He throws it back on to the table. "Piece of crap," he says.

This brings a sneer from the woman running the sale, who's already been giving him the creeps. She's dressed head to toe in bright, stretchy fabric that strains over her dark, doughy skin. He's already noticed she's missing several teeth. But the worst is the eye that's covered in a white film, like a cataract.

"Goodness," Sidney says. He's holding something grotesque at arm's length, something that flips a switch deep inside of Charlie, makes him want to recoil. It's a hand or something? Something shrunken and brown and hairy.

"What is that?" Charlie says.

"A paw, maybe?" Sidney says.

"Is monkey," Creep-erella says, having moved in close enough for Charlie to smell her breath. Her good eye is locked on him, unwavering. "Is custom in my country. Ten dollars."

"What would anyone want a monkey paw for?" Sidney says. He moves behind where she can't see him, pantomimes the paw scratching his balls.

"Is for luck" the woman says. "Five dollars."

That's when Charlie remembers the story from his childhood. "The Monkey's Paw". It's about a cursed paw that grants wishes to its owner, but they're wishes that come at an enormous price.

"Luck, right," Charlie says. Bad luck is more like it. "No thanks." He moves on to the next pile of crap.

Before they leave, Sidney's gathered up a sweater, a lamp, and the sequined top, just for giggles. "Maybe one day I'll have the boobs to pull this off," he jokes.

"Be careful what you wish for," Charlie jokes back.

While his brother is paying, Charlie has just enough time to find the paw once again, to stroke a finger across its leathery flesh. And even though it ends badly in the story, he can't help it, he's wishing the wish big and loud inside his head.

When he sets the paw back down, the woman's staring at him again, and she's grinning a twisted and toothless grin.

***

In the days that follow, anything is apt to trigger Charlie's depression: a phrase he hears on television, the random photograph of Mildred he finds tucked away in a book, a whiff of the rose-scented perfume he still hasn't had the strength to get rid of. When those feelings hit, he can do nothing but be swept along in the powerful undertow, dragged out to the black ocean where he claws like a swimmer for the surface.

Over time, those moments happen less, and on certain days, he's able to find the light.

Just like Dr. Holman tells him, life doesn't end.

On certain days, Charlie even starts to feel human again.

***

The morning it happens, he's sitting on the couch, thinking about Mildred. Actually, he's thinking about her garden. He hasn't been out there since that day. The weeds will be growing like wild, ruining everything she worked so hard for. It seems disrespectful, somehow.

He trudges in his slippers through the damp grass, stands in the very spot she fell. First thing he notices is, yes, the weeds have taken over. Last spring's plants are struggling for real estate.

But there's something else.

Some kind of weed he's never seen before. And it's borne fruit. A pod. The plant is sagging under its weight.

He stoops down to get a better look.

He's never seen anything like it. The pod's skin is smooth, with hourglass curves that seem feminine. The triad of green impressions on one end doesn't help either. They almost look like a face.

He lifts the pod with a finger, sees something else that's weird. Deep under the deep green flesh is a network of bluish squiggles.

He takes a closer look, sees some kind fluid surging inside of them. Pulsing in rhythm.

Like a heartbeat.

He can't help it; he vomits up his breakfast.

It takes him a moment to catch his breath. Then he reaches down, connects his fingers around the pod's dewy flesh, and snaps it.

Something crunches inside, like delicate bones breaking, and two of the green spots flutter open. Underneath, the color is shining and black, like the eyes of a spider. And then he hears it, a kind of high-pitched screeching.

He pulls the plant from the earth, tosses it across the yard. His hands tremble when he pulls the back door open, and he can't seem to get it closed fast enough.

***

The days that follow aren't easy. He fights his way through sleepless nights and becomes angry when the sun rises too quickly. He's in the garden before his coffee even, checking for the weed to grow back. It wants to: an eager sprig bursts through the soil every few days. Charlie pulls it up before it has a chance to thrive.

He doesn't know what it is, really. But he knows how it got there.

The paw.

In the story, a couple on the verge of poverty uses the first of the paw's three wishes on a sum of money, which leads to the accidental death of their only son. Their grieving hearts use the second wish to give him life again. The son returns, but not how they expected. His mangled body rises from the grave and knocks on their door. At least that's what's implied. There's no way of knowing who's knocking that fateful evening, because the father realizes what's happening and wishes the son dead again before his wife can open the door.

And now the same paw—or another one exactly like it—was working its own brand of horror in Charlie's life.

The paw. It never gives you what you wanted, not outright. You had to accept its "gift" on its terms. Something the couple in the story had been too terrified to do.

Talk to Sidney about it? Right. His brother would only call Dr. Holman. Or he'd want to see proof. Charlie won't bring him into this twisted little nightmare. Sidney's been through enough lately. And Charlie, he brought this on himself.

For these reasons, he never says anything to anyone.

There's something else, though.

Secretly, he wonders what would happen if he let the plant grow.

***

The ground is soggy from days of rain, so he doesn't visit the garden. At least, that's what he tells himself.

"I'm fine," he lies to Sidney on the phone. In truth, he's irritable from lack of sleep. He's drinking now to cope, something Dr. Holman would definitely not approve of. Three vodkas and he's out, for a few hours anyway.

Tonight, it's the fourth glass that does him in. That, and the pattering of the rain on the lawn. He passes out on the sofa watching *Nightline*.

He's lost in an unmemorable dream when he wakes up to a sound. It takes him a few seconds to remember where he is, and a few more to realize what's happening. The sound he hears is the patio door sliding open, grating against its frame.

His heart hammers into his chest, and he squeezes his eyes shut again. Although every instinct tells him to get up, to get out, fear keeps him frozen in place.

He can only listen to what might be footsteps, a kind of sloshing, dragging, sloshing sound on the carpet. Whatever is moving is large, and it's heavy and it's wet. The footsteps shuffle close, and he can hear breathing. Short ragged breaths, like an animal. It smells unwholesome and foul, like rotting vegetation.

There's another scent too. A soft, rosy note he recognizes immediately.

The sofa depresses next to him, and a viscous mouth clasps down over his. He yields with his lips, opens up to the flood of moist humus surging in, warm with the process of decay and twisting with the bodies of earthworms. He opens wider as the avalanche works its way past his tonsils, into his throat, his lungs, and when his eyes flicker

24

open, he understands finally, after all this time, what Mildred loved about the dirt.

***

He lies on the floor in the dim morning light all foggy headed, wondering where's she's gone. He wants to get up, but his body won't respond. It's like a wire's gone loose inside of him. From somewhere in the languid shadows, he hears that breathing again, and for a long moment he listens to its slow, erratic rhythm, feeling strangely at peace.

Until the itching starts.

It's the slightest sensation deep inside his chest. So faint at first, he wonders if he's imagined it.

Something has sprouted.

Whatever she put there has taken root. Somehow, he knows this. He feels it worming its way into his body. Burrowing into his soft parts. Growing like a cancer. There's pain as cells rupture, as whatever it is sinks tiny filaments into his organs. He feels a draining sensation, like he's being sucked dry from the inside out.

Or replaced, maybe.

Then he's in agony.

His dehydrated limbs contort, bending back on themselves at impossible angles. His elbow and knees crack as his joints give way. Gasping, he struggles for air, but even his lungs seem to be failing him. In defiance of the pain, he tries to clench his hands into fists, but it's more than his breaking body can bear. He can only stare at the useless appendages, watch wide-eyed as tiny green fibers thread their way through his flesh.

She shuffles out of the shadows.

Dark eyes stare at him from the leafy folds of her face. The open maw of her mouth crawls with insects: grubs, beetles, mayflies. In the cracks of her vegetal skin, he can see the scaffolding of vines that form her skeleton. From one of these fissures, a pair of mating ladybugs emerges, then plummets to the floor in apparent ecstasy.

When he hears her croaking voice it's with ears that are no longer fully human. "Grow..."

His body has no choice but to obey.

A surge of vitality courses through his body, as his broken limbs elongate, his fingers twist into gnarled digits. Dozens of sprigs break through the flesh on his back, enlarging, lengthening until their tips scrape the ceiling. His teeth clatter to the floor in bloody clumps, as new ones emerge, dozens of them, razor-sharp and hard as thorns. Out of his torso, new root-like legs probe downward, push through the crackling floorboard, into the dank air of the crawlspace, settling as if with a sigh into the moist earth below.

He knows the transformation is over when the last leaves have settled into place, rustling faintly like a tree on a summer morning.

Strangely, he's at peace, a feeling which intensifies when the first golden rays peep through the window.

She joins him at last in the warmth. Her hands rake through his limbs eagerly, searching, until she finds what she is looking for. With clumsy fingers, she seizes the bulb of his sex organ, which grows instantly rigid. She shoves it roughly into the flowering bud between her legs and in moments he's exploding inside her.

Spent, his tangled arms hold her. Already the fruit of their love is forming on her body, little buds maturing into pods, so many of them, so quickly. The dutiful mother disengages, lumbers out the back door, into the garden, where she begins placing them one by one into the earth.

Their children.

He watches until the hunger starts, bright and intense, unlike any he's ever known before. He thrusts his roots deeper into the soil, seeking nutrients, finding scant amounts, not enough. It hurts, this hunger. It's like he's dying. He wants to call to her, to tell her he doesn't want this, to beg her to change him back, when he hears a sound, familiar somehow. The jingling of keys in a lock. The creaking of an opening door.

And then a voice. "Charlie?"

It's a voice he knows, maybe? Some distant part of him wants to remember.

The intruder enters, stops for a moment when he sees the tangle of greenery, and then begins pushing through. Charlie can feel the assault on his limbs, the snapping and cracking of vines. And there's something else. In the new cells of his body, he can taste a cloud of molecules floating in the air. Fear, he thinks. The stranger's.

It's a suspicion that's verified when the intruder's stunned eyes lock onto the thing that used to be his brother.

Sidney, Charlie tries to say, but his mouth won't work for all the teeth. His powerful arms constrict, draw his brother toward him. A terrible sound fills the room, (screaming, perhaps?) but it ends with a crunch inside his powerful jaws.

There is food now, yes. Sticky and warm, dripping like the sweetest juice down his chin. There's an abundance. Plenty for him, for Mildred, for their babies.

Food enough for them all.

The many-limbed thing drags the slumped figure through the house and out to the garden, where his wife awaits, where his children are sprouting, tender green filaments silhouetted against the moist brown earth, reaching like hopeful angels toward the blue ocean sky.

GHOSTS ON DRUGS

You know the ghosts were in your apartment the minute you open the door, even before you've had a chance to loosen the tie that's been choking you all day. The stench of marijuana hits you in the face. The nerve of them, partying in your apartment while you were out selling cheap-ass suits.

The evidence is everywhere. You see depressions on the couch—ghost butt prints, what a fright. There are roaches in the ashtray, little seeds in the carpet, bits of crinkly ash on the table. They drank all your schnapps, moved on to the mouthwash, got into your medicine cabinet. They even took the pills Kimber got for the dog.

Bastards.

It fucks your head, to tell the truth. It fucks it good, and then you pace the floor and chain-smoke all night. So you oversleep, yeah, miss the radio alarm that's been set to the morning news. It's set that way because, since the nag left with the dog, you need the second-most-irritating sound in the world to get you out of bed in the mornings. It's not until you're dreaming about a hurricane in Honduras that's actually the big news story of the day that you realize the sun is too bright. You've overslept, again. So you get up, roll in to work three hours late.

Thanks for nothing, fucking ghosts.

Your boss is waiting, eager to write you up. He wants you to sign a slip. You reach for the pen in your pocket, but it's gone. Stupid ghosts probably used it to smoke meth or something. He hands you the pen from behind his ear, and you say, "Okay." The pen is greasy from that shit in his hair, and you can't get to the bathroom fast enough. You wash your hands in hot water, scrubbing and squeezing until they're red and raw, and then you feel like a dummy.

Burned hands are not okay.

They're making your life a mess, these ghosts. Nothing can stop them when they're on a bender.

***

The fuckers got smart last night. They unplugged your alarm clock so you wouldn't wake up and catch them.

You wake up anyway when you hear them clanking around in the living room. You almost surprise one too, but he vanishes into the walls, leaves behind a scorched glass pipe. There's a smoky haze in the air, torn squares of foil everywhere, all grimy and smeared. There are smudges on the furniture, an aluminum can ripped open on the table, tiny drops of blood where one of them cut his finger. Ha ha, fuckers.

It's almost noon, so you call work, tell them you're on your way. Your boss tells you not to bother. "Take some time," he says. "Decide if you really want to work here."

You don't, of course, but you don't need him to know that. So you say, "Okay."

***

It's gotten worse.

They've been here every day this week. Your apartment, it's a mess. Dirty dishes are piled everywhere, and the garbage is stuffed to overflowing. The air is muggy and dank, and the carpet smells like piss, and not just in the bathroom.

Then there are the oily spots. Transparent smears all over the apartment, so gross. Their jacked-up heartbeats make them ooze ghost grease on whatever they touch. The doorjambs. The table. The remotes.

Especially the remotes.

They like to watch your dirty movies.

You know this because DVD cases are everywhere. Skin rags flipped open on the couch, on the floor. Ripped pages all around. Random girl parts cut out with scissors, reassembled on the table. Composite girls with perfect tits, perfect asses, perfect smiles. You find Kleenex wads stuck to the carpet, crusty washcloths in the hamper.

Jesus, what to do, what to do?

***

You catch one finally, in the bathroom, when you turn on the light. He's standing in front of you, a pasty ghoul with open sores and wild eyes glaring out from darkened sockets. Your heart flips, but when you look again, he's gone. It's just you, staring at the mirror.

Why are they here, you wonder?

Or are they here?

They're making you miserable. You hope they don't come tomorrow, okay.

***

These ghosts are going to be the death of you.

Maybe it's time do something.

You look up therapy groups online and find one for depressed adults. Oh, joy. You stand in a room full of strangers and you talk about stupid shit—like the people you've wronged, the things you wished you hadn't done but did, the things you wished you'd done differently. You go to two different meetings and you drink bad coffee and stare at your watch and think they're all a bunch of idiots.

Then on your third visit, they ask you to talk.

And you're like, ummm, shit. But then something breaks like an egg inside of you and all those tender pieces you've been ignoring spill out. So you tell them everything.

Everything.

To a room full of fucking strangers.

They listen.

And listen.

When it's over, they're on you like maggots on a piece of chicken. "It's okay," they say, all awkward hugs and cold coffee smiles. "You can change, if you want." Slowly, you start to believe them.

So you go back to your apartment. It doesn't take long to gather up the stuff—the pills, the weed, the booze—and throw it in the dumpster. You even wave to the garbage man when he hauls it all away. He just looks at you funny.

It's not easy, not at all. You get the shakes for three days straight. You scratch sores into your face with all your nervous energy. You cry yourself to sleep more than once. It's tough, damn it, but you make it, somehow. Weather out the storm, so to speak.

And then, something amazing.

You stop feeling like crap all the time. Your skin clears up. You put weight back on.

But the best thing?

No more ghosts.

Which means you're sleeping better. So the mornings don't hurt like they used to. You do push-ups in the living room just because it feels good. It's not long before you work up the nerve to strut down to the store, talk your boss into giving you your job back.

Even Kimber's back in the picture, sort of. Just phone calls, for now. But maybe more soon? Her voice doesn't annoy you like it used to. If anything, you decide it's got a musical quality, is actually kind of beautiful. She does silly stuff that makes you laugh. Like put the dog on the phone so you can talk to him. You make your voice real high and you do kissy noises and you say dumb things like who's a good boy, but the dumb little shit doesn't get it. All he does is pant, pant, pant into the phone.

But you don't mind it much, really.

You don't mind it much at all.

***

Weeks later, your team hits a big sales quota at work. Your boss is a gorilla, all chest thumps and whoots. When the store closes, everyone is pumped, you all decide to go out to a bar. The drinks help you all pretend to like each other. It's beer-whisky-beer, whisky-beer-whisky, and then you're feeling pretty damn good. Better than you've felt for months, probably. You drink until they all load into taxis like a bunch of clowns, and you wave good night, tell them the night air will do you some good. The moon is glowing like a meteor from another dimension, like it's giving you powers or something, and you barely feel the sidewalk under your feet. Maybe you're flying? All you know is you don't want it to end.

It doesn't have to, a voice inside of you says, so you reach for your pocket and pull out your phone.

***

Next, its hours later.

You're standing at your front door, and you think, oh shit.

You'd recognize that smell anywhere.

Inside, it's a raging ghost party. There's got to be fifty of the fuckers here—deadheads and sluts, hipsters and rockers. The music is blaring and everybody's talking loud and they're laughing and they're cussing. "Where you been?" one of the ghosts says, leading you inside.

They're up to no good, fucking ghosts. They're guzzling liquor out of paper cups, screwing on your furniture. There's goddamn drugs everywhere. You see them in plastic baggies, in dirty foil wrappers, in fluffy piles on the table. They're doing it in every way imaginable. Snorting it noisily through straws. Rubbing it on their lips. Smoking it in their shiny glass pipes.

Someone shoves a bong in your face.

You think, fuck it, and take a long, slow drag. Why not? You figure. It's just one night.

The buzz, it's like, damn... wait, what were we talking about? Ha, ha. Now your worries are slipping away. Soon, all you care about is the drinking, the smoking, the mother-fucking party, man. You're at it all night with your new friends—I said all damn night, baby—until the sun comes up, shits all over everything. That's when somebody passes around a bottle of pills, little, tiny red ones, and you wolf down a handful. It's not long until you're drowsy and drift off to sleep.

And sleep.

And sleep.

Next thing you know someone's pounding on the door. You're too tired to give a fuck, though. Sleep, that's what you need. Silence. That soothing deadness.

***

A key rattles in the door. You open your eyes to find—

Wait, what are you seeing? The perspective's all wrong.

Kimber's in your apartment, but it's like you're hovering above her, like the action is happening under your feet. She's red-faced and ugly crying, just hysterical, a mess. Damn, you've never seen the nag so upset. She's kneeling over some sleeping dude and slapping his face and crying. She's telling him to get up, get up, you piece of shit, goddammit. She's got the dog with her. And a fucking policeman, too. Christ, almighty.

Then it hits you.

That dude...

He's you.

There's no time to dwell on it, because your new friends are here now—your ghost friends. Pretty soon there's a beer in your hand, and the party's raging all over again. You all sit there and watch the scene with Kimber like it's a goddamed TV show. When the paramedics show up to cart off your body, you're making commentary like it's *Mystery Science Theater 3000* or something. It's hysterical.

You think you'll miss her a little, Kimber. The dog, maybe more.

But hey, it's not like you're going to be alone. You've got these awesome new friends. A whole apartment full of them. You're going to be together for a long time. At a party that'll last forever.

Maybe being dead isn't such a bad thing, you think.

At least you don't have to sell cheap-ass suits anymore, okay.

MUMBO JUMBO

The last place he thought he'd meet the Devil was in Arkansas, with its silver lakes and vigorous hills, the land itself like a blessing from God. But she smiled like a Buddhist and love took root despite the peculiar things he soon discovered. Like the dolls in her closet with pins in their eyes, and her tendency to collect spider webs, rolling them into a ball the way his grandmother kept rubber bands.

Then: the night he found her in the backyard with lightning flickering in her hair and bats circling her head like harpies. She was chanting strange words in a language he didn't know, some weird mumbo jumbo. He coaxed her inside and how she lit up with passion then. She was a terrorist with his flesh, raking his back with her fingernails, the fury of her love like lasers on his skin, forcing him to bleed into the bedclothes—red, so much red everywhere, the color of danger, of warning lights and emergency exits. He tried to escape, but she called out in that strange mumbo jumbo and then she was coming like rockets in a voice that wasn't hers, a tarantula wasp stinging him over and over with bliss.

***

In the days after, she clung to him like a remora and he found himself unable to scrape her from the underbelly of his life. At night, he watched her creep out the window. Always, she returned before dawn, naked with mud in her toes and panting like a dog, her soft skin shivering like milk against his, ravenous for love. And oh how he tried but her carrion breath repulsed him until he sprang from the bed in horror. Then she spoke in that strange mumbo jumbo, becoming his queen once more, her pink flesh chanting his name like a psalm. Obediently, he knelt for communion, her voice sedating his fears while he probed her tender folds. And: finding maggots against his tongue, all of them suckling at her softness, her fat squirming children, their single black eyes twitching, bodies pulsing with her wrath. And him, screaming screaming screaming and running for the door while her siren voice called out mumbo jumbo mumbo jumbo mumbo jumbo. He returned to her, dutiful servant that he was, and next thing he knew he was mounting her like a lion, her teeth ripping him open, his blood falling like rain on his chest. What powers did she possess? he wondered in the palpitating light as her shadow became a dragon and thunder shook the house.

The next day he woke with wounds in his skin. So many scars, scratched into him like a message. When he tried to read them the mumbo jumbo in his head pounded his thoughts to gristle.

***

One afternoon she lay down for a nap.

In his despair, he knew what he had to do. Knife flashing at his side, he slipped into her room. An inkblot of doubt plagued him when he saw her asleep. Then working quickly, he covered her face with a sheet. The knife jerked up for its fatal swing but stopped suddenly at the sound of her laughter, that hideous mumbo jumbo. His will draining like bathwater, he fell to the floor, his weapon clattering next to his head, useless and impotent. She coiled around him like a python, her ancient eyes gleaming. With the slash of a razor talon, she opened him up, the sheets darkening like chum clouds in shark-infested waters. Then, as she screamed and laughed, those shining claws did their work, burrowing away pieces of him bit by bit, clumps of his flesh pelting the lampshade, his blood splattering the ceiling.

"Flesh is the devil," he sobbed as her leathery wings enfolded him.

IN THE NIGHT, A WHISPER

1

A darkened street on Halloween night. A throng of children follow an adult with a flashlight, their shoes clopping on the sidewalk, all of them giggling, shouting, merry. Costumes flap, rustle, jingle. Flashes of color: gold, white, silver, blue. A skinny skeleton smooths his sleeve, a pint-sized robot steadies an antenna on her head. They carry items to collect their loot: a plastic pumpkin, a shopping bag, a pillowcase. The yellow blob of the flashlight sweeps the lawns glistening with evening dew. All are too occupied to notice the dark figure in the shadows of a hedge. She watches them silently, stealthily before slipping into the group.

2

Her costume is specifically chosen. A scarlet smock pulled from her mother's closet, slightly threadbare and faded. Her dark wiry hair is pulled into a bun to keep it out of her eyes. A waist-length cape flutters on her back. The mask is plastic and cheap, an item she begged for at the drugstore. It conceals the top of her face except her steely blue eyes, which stare out beneath two snaggy horns. Along the mask's bottom, a row of jagged teeth stretches over her own mouth, giving her an infernal, frightening grin. Her sneakers are dusty, the soles as smooth as a cat's belly.

3

\

She blends in without fanfare, without protest, without the batting even of an eye. Deftly, foxily, cunningly, she keeps pace with them on the sidewalk, her feet shuffling with theirs, as silent as a whisper. Soon, it's like she'd always been there. Not all of the children know each other. Trick or treating is a communal occasion, the more the merrier. Their costumes make it difficult to keep track of everyone, anyway.

4

At every door, the same mantra is heard: "Trick or treat! Smell my feet! Give me something good to eat!"

5

Swooping from door to door, they hunt for confections like flies seeking honey. Their thoughts are of red licorice ribbons, long as their forearms and as supple as rubber bands. Of vibrant hard candies that fizz their tongues like soda. Of fruity jellies dusted with sparkling sugar crystals. Of warm caramel globs smudging the corners of their mouths. Of fragrant chocolate bars melting on their fingers. Of the satisfying crunch of malt balls. Of sticky brittle clinging like cement to their molars. Of the achy zing of lemon drops on their tastebuds. Of giant sweet lollies that last all day and stain their lips crimson, violet, emerald.

6

Doors swing open. Oohs, ahhhs, gasps. The procession transpires with serpentine precision. Candies drop into bags, thunk, thunk, thunk.

7

"Oh, look at you sweet little things! Happy Halloween to you all! What's this, a pirate! How jolly. With a hook for a hand, no less. I hope you gave that crocodile a good what for! Here, have some toffee and a cinnamon stick. A vampire! Such makeup. Truly frightening. Here you go, here you go. And here! A precious little princess. Three pieces for you dear—shhh, it's our secret. And you, Mr. Doctor. Is the stethoscope your father's? You must tell him to lower my bill. And oh! Lookit this little girl. Or is she a witch? Who knows, who knows? Happy Halloween to you, sweetie. And here! A wizard! With a magic wand, to boot. How quaint! And who's this holding up the rear? A cat girl? No, my mistake. A devil, perhaps? My, that's a scary mask, dear. Did you make it yourself? Oh, a quiet one, I see. Didn't your mother tell you it's rude not to answer your elders? And it wouldn't hurt you to smile dear. It's Halloween, after all, my goodness. One piece for you, now off you go, you odd little thing. Next year, try not to take yourself so seriously."

8

In the crowd, she walks next to this child, then that one. Her gaze returns to the boy in the ghost costume. Even without seeing his expression, his eyes tell her everything. He's awkward around others, a little nervous, probably a bit of a loner. Perfect.

9

For the boy in the ghost costume, it's his best night ever. Under the white sheet, a grin crinkles his face, his round cheeks flush in the cool air. His pulse is quick, excited. The plastic bag in his hand, nearly half-full, swells pleasantly. His gaze jumps nimbly from the glowing full moon to the spooky lawn decor, to the remaining doors on the block, to the passing groups of children, so many, so many. He is wondering if his treats will last 'til Christmas when there's a tap on his shoulder.

10

"You like candy?" "Oh yes, so much." "I know a place that has lots of it. The good stuff. Better than here." "Like what?" "Like cream eggs and Bon Bons and candy cigarettes and cupcakes as big as your hand." "Where?" "Just a few streets over. Follow me." "Mm, I don't know." "No risk, no reward. What are you, a fraidy cat?"

11

He follows, dreaming of butterscotch clusters and nougat bars. His mouth waters, anticipating the heady rush of sugar in his body. Onward she leads him, around a corner, through an alley, into another neighborhood. When he looks up again, the streets are dark, the houses are ugly, unfamiliar. An owl hoots overhead. Where are his companions, he wonders? Their laughter has died away.

12

"Jump, already," says the girl in the devil costume. She sits on her haunches on the other side of the gully. He shifts uneasily, gauging the distance—ten feet that seem like a mile. He stares down past the steep drop below where a creek burbles through a rocky bed. It's a good fall if he misses, with nothing to slow his descent except vines, trash, weeds. "You sure it's safe?" he whines over the lump in his throat. "What if I don't make it?" "You will," she laughs. "If I can do it, so can you." A running jump, that's all he needs. He takes a few steps back, inhales deeply, the muscles in his young legs coiled like springs.

13

So close, she thinks, he's so close to doing it! She eases forward to watch, trying to keep a straight face. When he misses, the fool, when he falls and he plummets, she will look away. Nor will she gaze down at his young body shattered against the boulders. She's not a monster, after all. Just lonely, just bored, wanting someone to play with. Jump! Jump! JUMP!

14

Searing light fills the eyeholes in his costume, a hand pulls him back by his scruff. "Bobby!" the adult with the flashlight scolds. "Didn't you hear me calling?" The boy gapes wide-eyed into the light and blinks as if waking from a dream. "What on earth are you doing?" "Following her," he says, pointing across the chasm at the girl. Of course, nobody's there.

15

"I hate you," she'd screamed at her mother through the thin bedroom door. Grounded! On Halloween night. If only she hadn't talked back when she'd been asked to take out the trash. But where was the fun in that? By that time in her young life, sarcasm had become a habit, a defense mechanism, a way of existence. Damn! She simply *had* to go trick or treating. Especially when she'd worked so hard on her costume.

So, she'd locked her bedroom door. Turned the radio up loud. Crawled into the smock. Tied on the mask, the cape. While Ritchey Valens sang "Donna", she crept out the window and into the darkness. Within an hour, every door on her street was visited. Her candy bag felt heavy, threatening to burst.

16

The officer knelt under a great gnarled tree. He shook his head at the body, such a shame to lose them so young. Her costume reminded him of his own daughter at home, and he grieved silently for her parents. In a puddle nearby, the devil mask lay soaked. Around the girl's neck, dark bruises mottled the flesh.

17

She was heading home, her head held high and a satisfied grin on her face when the old station wagon pulled up beside her. Lost in her thoughts, she barely cared at all—until the car stopped. The door opened. A large man bounded in front of the headlights. In one brutal instant, everything changed. A rough calloused hand clamped over her mouth. Strong hairy arms ensnared her. The stench of his sweat filled her nose. She flailed, kicked, and scratched, but ultimately was forced in the car.

18

She watches the yellow blob of light recede with blue murky eyes. A shudder passes through what's left of her heart. She wrings her hands together, as if to massage away the disappointment. She removes the mask, soaks the smock with her tears. Next year she will try again. Until then she will walk the streets alone, a wraith in the shadows, her only company the moon, the owls, the darkness. Her head drops into her hands, and she huddles under a rotting elm. Above her and all around, the night's shadows creep, gnaw, devour. Her bony shoulders quake with sadness, with shame, with loneliness.

EVIL, INC.
(OR HOW TO SUCCEED IN BUSINESS WITHOUT REALLY DYING)

Brian knows he's in for it the second he steps into his boss's office, plunging him smack dab into a conversation between the firm's two highest-ranking executives. Immediately, he wishes he'd kept the news about the backed-up men's room toilet to himself. It's too late, though. His mouth is a waterfall, and the words are spilling out.

Mr. Jackson's not happy about the interruption, obviously. He fixes his steely gaze on Brian and flings the report he's reading to the desk with an angry slap. From under his desk, he pulls out a jar of maple syrup. It's of the finest quality, he often brags, flown in from Vermont at considerable expense. Brian senses his day is ruined when Mr. Jackson globs a fingerful of the stuff onto his lips. Everyone around the office knows this strange ritual is how he begins his legendary ass chewings. "Mr. Gray," Mr. Jackson says with a smack. "Haven't you unclogged a toilet before?"

Brian feels his nuts crawl up inside his crotch.

He's got no one to blame but himself, really. He should have learned by now not to engage the two men on days they've spent time in their private meeting room. Whatever they got up to behind that red door down the hall, it always got them in a nasty mood, today being no exception.

"Yes, sir," Brian offers. "But you hired me to be an accountant."

Mr. Jackson rises swiftly for his age and closes the distance between them. "You'd rather we call maintenance, then? Pass the buck when an able man could solve the problem in a moment's time?" He's so close, Brian can smell maple on his breath.

"But, sir, that's not my job," Brian says.

"*Not my job*," Mr. Jackson mocks. "Can you believe it, Dudley?"

Brian tries to catch Mr. Cady's eye, but the vice-president only looks down at the top of his expensive shoes, as if he's being ever so thoughtful about other, more important matters.

"That's the problem these days," Mr. Jackson continues. "Employees have no sense of dedication. Well, let me teach you a thing or two about that."

Next, Brian is working a plunger in the stinking toilet while Mr. Jackson shouts orders from behind. "Put your back into it," he barks. "Give us some of that can-do American spirit."

It's a weird situation, made even weirder when the old man starts singing the "Battle Hymn of the Republic".

Brian does his best to ignore the old man's taunts, the singing. If he had any more courage, he'd shove the old bastard against the wall, tell him to fuck off. But what can he do? Retirement is still ten years away, and there's that pension to think about.

So he takes it.

"His truth is mar-ching on!" sings Mr. Jackson, just as Brian dislodges the stubborn turd, splashing filthy water onto his shirt, his shoes.

There's a sharp peal of laughter from Mr. Jackson, a slap on the back. "Well done."

On the way back to the office, Brian dabs at his shirt with a paper towel. It had been a hell of a year since the two bigwigs had taken over the company. Since then, Alta Marketing had been through its share of changes. There was the rebranding, the name change to Kaos, Inc., the downsizing, the layoffs. But the efforts had succeeded. The firm had rebounded from bankruptcy and was even thriving. Revenue was stronger than it had been in years.

But at what cost? The new bosses were prone to mood swings—particularly Mr. Jackson. Brian's self-esteem, which had never been a strength, had eroded almost to the point of self-loathing.

More, the remaining employees often talked about the sense of dread that had taken over the office. Those who worked late into the evenings reported feeling like they were being watched. Or they saw things. Shadows moving in unoccupied rooms. Doors that slammed mysteriously shut. And then there was that strange smoky smell that wafted through the office occasionally, seemingly out of nowhere.

Back in the office, Mr. Cady is waiting by the red door, tapping his watch. Brian's about to ask if he can run home for a change of clothes, but Mr. Jackson beats him to the punch. "Get me the Jaxon report," he says, waving his card in front of the magnetic reader. "Like, yesterday." The door creaks open and the two executives disappear into the inky darkness.

Brian gets to work. The rest of the day, there's a vague scent of human waste clinging to his clothes. The smell starts off as an annoyance but builds into a pounding headache. He's miserable by the time he prints out the final report on crisp, white paper—no creases or marks, per strict orders—and places them on Mr. Jackson's desk.

There's no one else in the office; it's way after closing time. He takes a moment for himself, presses his forehead against the cool glass to soothe away the day's tension.

Below, people scurry about on the street like ants. Surely none of them would notice if he slid open the window and eased out onto the ledge. If he closes his eyes, he can see himself out there, leaning against the wall, the wind ruffling what's left of his balding hair. In the distance, he can hear waves crashing against some rocky shore. Which is impossible, he knows. The closest beach is hours away. Still, he hears it. The sound is soothing, hypnotic. The longer he listens, the more he sees himself stepping out into nothingness, falling, middle fingers raised defiantly as salvation rises to greet him.

But he doesn't have the courage today.

He opens his eyes to find a stony gargoyle on the ledge. The grotesque face stares out into the night, its eyes bulging, its bat-like ears cocked like antennas tuned to Brian's existential agony. Brian wishes for the statue to come alive, to spread its mighty wings and become airborne, to feast its insatiable appetite on this whole horrible town and everyone in it.

It doesn't, though.

But the unwholesome thought lingers as he locks up for the night and hurries past the awful red door. It's haunting him still minutes later when he thinks he hears, somewhere in the murky shadows far above the city, the flapping of leathery wings.

***

The text from Mr. Jackson comes in just before midnight: *See you at 8 a.m. sharp!* which means Brian spends the rest of the night staring at the ceiling. He chugs too much black coffee and walks to work jittery and nervous.

At the office, he's settling in with another coffee he doesn't need when Mr. Jackson plops down on the edge of his desk. He's in a mood, Mr. Jackson. The morning's lecture is about outsourcing this, cutting expenses that. At least that's what Brian thinks he's talking about. He can't really concentrate because of the bug.

It's been crawling across the window for the past few minutes, a coal-black insect with red compound eyes. He thinks it's an ant, maybe, except it's huge, the size of his finger. He's only seen ants this big in nature films, but never one quite like this. The long, toothed mandibles. The spines extending the length of its back.

He's wondering how such a nasty thing got up so high, when a pigeon lands on the ledge. The bird cocks its head, blinks its dirty yellow eyes. Next thing Brian knows, it's flying off, the bug twitching in its beak.

The commotion makes it hard to focus on Mr. Jackson's diatribe about "the bottom line," especially when the bird lets out a squawk loud enough to hear through the double panes of glass. There's a fluttering of wings, a spray of gray feathers. The bird plummets like a stone.

"Gray?" Mr. Jackson asks. "You getting all this?"

Brian turns away from the scene. "Loud and clear."

"Any questions?"

Lots, Brian thinks. Like what about the poor people in the media department who are about to be laid off? He's known some of them for years. Like Jerry Loftis, who's finally scraped together enough money with his wife to make a down payment on their dream home. And Enid Kelava, a divorced immigrant with a special-needs son who works harder than anyone he knows. Brian thinks, *what about them, you callous son of a bitch?*

What he says is: "Are we sure there's no other way?"

"Rabbits," Mr. Jackson says, rising.

"Pardon?"

"The world is a savage place, Gray, and it's filled with two types of people. On the one hand, you've got rabbits." He curls his index fingers over his temples, bucks his teeth. "Rabbits are helpless creatures. They live in holes, afraid of everything.

"And then there are lions, Gray. The hungry-hearted. Lions are the doers in this world. They're mighty because it is their birthright. You follow?"

Brian nods, yeah, he gets it.

"So if you're a hungry lion, and you see a rabbit hopping by, you going to sit there and starve? Hell, no! You're going to pounce on that sucker, eat until you've had your fill. So, which of these are you, Gray? A rabbit or a lion?"

"A lion, sir?"

Mr. Jackson dismisses him with the wave of a hand. "You asking me, or telling me?"

"I'm telling you, sir! I'm a lion."

Suddenly, Mr. Jackson is in Brian's space, his nose just inches away. "You'd best be, son. Let me tell you another thing. This company, it's a lion. Proud. Strong. It's that way because a few of us have made it so. Now, let's say you have a department full of rabbits. Oh, take media, for instance. Losers who can't hit their numbers. A drag on the system. What kind of animal do you think they are?"

"R-rabbits?"

"Damn right, Gray. So don't let me think you feel pity for these people." He eases back, motions toward the phone. "Now do me a favor. Take your place among the pride."

Brian picks up the handset, notices his fingers are shaking. He thinks Mr. Jackson is going to sense his hesitation, rip the phone away, and shout the order into it himself.

But he doesn't.

When it's over, Brian waits before heading down to the fourth floor. Many have already gone. The ones who remain are slack-faced, stunned. They're clearing out their desks, packing their effects into cardboard boxes. Some, like Jerry Loftis, won't look him in the eye. "Don't let this get you down," Brian tells him. "You're smart. Something will turn up soon."

He's exhausted by the time he heads back to his office. The last thing he expects to hear is laughter in the hallway, but he hears it anyway. It's Mr. Jackson, on his way to the red room. Mr. Cady's just behind, a bottle of champagne and flute glasses gathered in his arms. "Ah! The man of the hour," Mr. Jackson says. "Fancy a toast?"

Brian shakes his head.

"Suit yourself." Mr. Jackson clicks the door open. "The first time is always the hardest. You'll come to realize that corporate life is a rollercoaster, all ups and downs. Try not to hang on to the bar too tight, Gray. It's a lot more fun when you just let go."

Brian tries to work out how anyone could see this as fun while the two men disappear into the red room. He gives in to his curiosity and presses his ear against the door. He's not sure what he's expecting to hear. The sounds of celebration, maybe. Glasses clinking together. More of that cruel laugher, or whatever.

What's weird is, he hears nothing.

***

He's still feeling guilty a week later, a little. Some of it's lessened when the bosses fly to Japan for a meeting, leaving Brian in charge. It's a turn on, the power. In the afternoon, he places a call to Suki and sets up an appointment—she's a hooker he likes to call and he keeps her number on speed dial. The rest of the day, he can't stop thinking about the sex they're going to have. Maybe he'll keep his suit on tonight, play the part of the powerful executive dishing it out to the bad girl.

When she gets to his apartment, he's not feeling it. She's straddling him, rubbing her nipples across his back, which is normally enough to get him going, but he's distracted. For one, there's sand in the sheets. It's coarse, irritating. Had she gotten laid at some beach today and not had the decency to shower? And where around the city was there a beach with red sand?

She reaches underneath to give him a tug. "Feel good, baby?"

He says it does, it feels fine. Says he's just stressed, is all. If he could just turn his head off, he thinks, nature will take its course. Thirty minutes later she'll be tucking the money into her bra on the way out the door.

Tonight, though, the dough ain't rising.

She turns him over, nibbles on his neck. One of the things that always drives him crazy.

Nothing.

"You know," she whispers, "Normally we're at it like rabbits by now."

Rabbits.

The word opens a floodgate inside him, and now all he can do is think about work. About the incident in the toilet. The poor souls in the marketing department. All the lives affected by the layoffs. By something he was made to do.

She may as well have doused him in ice water.

What sucks is, he still has to pay her. "An hour's an hour," the girls always say. She won't even look at him when she leaves.

Terrible feeling, for a prostitute to think you're a bad lay.

He changes out the sheets for new ones, cusses up a storm when he finds there's sand in them too. Frustrated and angry, he sits in the gloomy silence for what feels like an hour, balling up the sheets with his fists, releasing them, balling them up again.

***

On day number two as Big Man in Charge, he's up and off to work early. Halfway through the alley, he hears someone urinating behind the dumpster. He tries to walk more quickly, but it's too late. The bum sees him.

He steps out into Brian's path, a wretch of a man in soiled clothes. "Yo, Magic Man," he says, fumbling with a broken zipper. "Got a dollar?"

Brian tries to avoid his gaze, notices the piss spot darkening the front of the guy's pants. "I'm in a hurry."

"Come on. Ain't eaten in two days."

The way he smells, Brian guesses, it's been longer since he's bathed. "Some other time."

"Fuck, man," the bum says.

Brian's caught off guard by the disappointing tone. He would have thought a panhandler would be used to rejection, but the hurt in his voice sounds genuine. It's only then that Brian takes a good look. The wreck of natty hair. The bags under the eyes. The filthy beard covering his neck and chin.

"Look," Brian says. "I'll give you a fiver if you can answer a question."

"Whatever."

"Why'd you call me 'Magic Man'?"

"Because look at you, man. Dope suit. New shoes. Bet you work in a fancy, air-conditioned office. Your life is magic, man. Compared to mine."

Magic? Hardly. If the bum knew what Brian's life was like. Degraded by his bosses. Barely able to keep up with his workload, no matter how many hours he puts in. Riddled by guilt, impotent.

It's laughable, really.

The bum sees the suit and thinks Brian's got it easy. He doesn't consider the responsibilities that come with it. The obligations. The pressures. It's stereotyping, plain and simple. Brian decides it's not worth losing five dollars over and turns to walk away.

"Yo, fuck you," the bum calls out.

Whatever. Brian's walking.

"Yeah, go back to your sweet office, your air conditioning. Ignore us poor bastards down here, sweating and starving. You entitled son of a bitch."

Brian stops, feels his face flushing. What a joke, to be judged by this shit-stain of a human being. The bum's misfortunes were a result of choices he'd made in life, just as surely as Brian had made his own. Only, instead of taking the hard road, this clown had taken the easy one. That's why he was living in this alley today.

Mr. Jackson had a term for people like this.

Rabbits.

Even later, Brian can't explain what came over him. How he felt the roar growing inside his chest. How he couldn't stop himself from springing toward the bum like a lion, all feral fury and muscle, spittle flying from his mouth, his fists pummeling.

When he finishes, the bum's a funhouse version of before. Lips split. Eyes swollen. Any facial symmetry forever erased. Brian's chest is pounding, and he feels woozy. Almost drunk.

He's still lightheaded when he enters the office, makes a beeline to a private bathroom. He wipes blood from his shoe, flicks away a bit of chipped tooth. It's a few moments before his breathing returns to normal. The high doesn't leave, though. It stays with him the rest of the day.

And he likes it.

At closing time, he drops off the daily report on Mr. Jackson's desk. And for some reason, his fingers make their way to the drawer. It's unlocked. He thumbs it open. There, next to the syrup jar, is a spare card key.

He disables the security cameras, slinks like a cat through the office.

He stands in front of the red door and pauses.

There's a feeling of inevitability inside of him. Like he's on the threshold of something, well, he doesn't know what. Something big.

Then the card passes in front of the reader, the door clicks open, and the darkness swallows him like a living thing.

***

When Brian comes to, he feels like he's vomited up his intestines. His first thought is, there's been a fire, because it's hot and there's smoke everywhere. Maybe he's passed out, he thinks. He starts to pull himself up, is surprised to find he's stretched out on a patch of sand, not linoleum or carpet. Hot sand, the color of blood, unlike anything he's ever seen.

He's not in the office. He's not anyplace he recognizes.

He's in—a desert?

There's red sand everywhere, humpbacked mounds of it, as far as he can see. Motes of ash drift through the smoky haze like dirty snow. Fumes sting his throat and burn his eyes. Above, strained light from twin red suns struggle to pierce the gloom.

He's thinking maybe he's lost it, bought himself a one-way ticket to the nuthouse, when the voice speaks. Or maybe it's many voices. He hears it, them, not in his ears, but directly in his head:

We've been expecting you, they say.

Because he doesn't know what else to do, he walks toward the voice, where he imagines its coming from. He walks a long time. The heat crashes down on him, his thirst growing with every step.

In the distance, he hears waves crashing on a beach. The sand he's walking on becomes dark with moisture, and ahead he sees an ocean. The water churns and roils in the heat. Smoke rolls across the beach like fog and rising out of it are two hunched figures. As he gets closer, he can make out leathery wings sprouting from their backs.

Horns jutting from their foreheads. Thin lips that barely cover the rows of jagged teeth.

Gargoyles.

One of them watches his approach. The other is playing like a cat with something in the smoke at its feet. The creature lifts its muscular arms, slashes them down again. Something wet whizzes past Brian's head and lands on the sand with a sickening slap. He tries to get a look at it, but already swarms of insects are surging out from under the sand to feast on whatever it was. The bugs, he's seen one before. On the window at the office.

He jabs at whatever it is they're eating with his foot. They scurry off enough for him to get a look.

It's skin.

The smoke curls away, revealing what the second beast has been playing with. It's a full heartbeat until Brian identifies the bloody pulp as a man. He's bound at the hands and feet, his skin torn away in ragged strips. Sand clings to the moisture on his blood-slicked body, and a dim light of awareness flickers in his eyes. He's still alive, but barely.

It's Mr. Cady.

One of the bugs has crawled up the first gargoyle's leg, onto his chest. The monster plucks the creature from its scaly flesh, holds it up to examine it. The flick of a claw eviscerates the bug, which squirts a yellowish fluid onto the sand. The gargoyle shrieks shrilly, a sound that Brian interprets as laughter, and flings the bug's carcass into the sand. The other insects move in quickly, shred the body into pieces.

Now, just beyond the gargoyle, Brian can see the other man.

It's Mr. Jackson. Stripped naked, forced to kneel in supplication. A plunger's been shoved handle-first into his rectum. He struggles against the cords that bind his hands and feet. He's struggling to cry for help through the gag in his mouth.

Then, for Brian, the agony comes.

Something's happening to his body. His bones are changing shape, some elongating, others shortening. He can feel his backbone bowing out, drawing him down into a hunched position. His skin is on fire, becoming scaly, darkening like old leather.

You are home now, the voices say. *In the land behind closed doors. Down here where the senses end. Chaos has you in its cage, all rusted and dusted in your wildest hour of pain.*

The second gargoyle moves closer, offers something to Brian. The pain in Brian's body is so intense, it's hard to make out what the object is. He doesn't have to see it, though. It's a jar of syrup. He can smell the maple from here. He reaches out to take the offering, but what he sees grabs the jar isn't a hand. It's a claw.

Some ancient and vast universe pushes its way into his brain, like a blanket the size of the world, smothering everything he knows. He struggles to break free, but it's no use. There's pressure, so much pressure, building up in his shoulder blades, finally releasing in a bright explosion of pain as the flesh yields and wings sprout from his back.

He is the lion, waiting in the grass.

He's on a rollercoaster, and he's letting go.

Already the syrup is pouring from the jar, anointing the naked flesh of the sniveling man at his feet.

It's feeding time.

HUNGRY WATERS

People aren't being mean when they ask. It's the kind of thing you'd expect to hear at a pool or lake when everyone else is in their swimsuits but you're standing there in your Bermuda shorts and loafers with your arms folded tightly across your chest:

"Aren't you getting in?"

It's been ten years since it happened, but tears always sting my eyes. I rarely answer. Instead, I look skyward and think of Corinne.

I was supposed to be watching her. That was the deal. Mom would drop us off at Poseidon's Playground, and I would look after my little sister. The water park was all the kids in town were talking about since its grand opening earlier that summer. My sister and I seemed to be the only ones who hadn't gone yet.

The wave pool, everyone said, was totally killer.

Before I go on, you shouldn't blame Mom. She was doing the best she could after Dad left. Sure, it was a holiday, but not for hotel workers. Someone had to change the sheets, fluff the pillows and clean the toilets.

I was fifteen, skinny and awkward with raging hormones. Corinne was seven, cute as a button with yellow hair and a Barbie obsession. It was the summer of 2024, the year SETI finally told the public they'd been receiving alien signals from outer space. Of course, they only said so afterwards. Had anyone known earlier, Corinne might still be—

No, there I go blaming again. If those years in therapy taught me anything, it's to take responsibility for my actions.

I...

Excuse me. It's still hard to talk about.

I was supposed to be watching her.

It was Labor Day, and the park was full of locals getting in their last soak of the season. The day was sweltering hot. Almost everyone was in the wave pool. I can still smell the suntan lotion and chlorine in the air, and as long as I live, I'll never forget the sight of all those people waiting for the machines to turn on, treading water in the deep end with their heads bobbing along the surface. Not Corinne, though. She was in the shallow end where I could watch her. I don't know that I'd ever seen her so happy, splashing around in her Barbie floaties, sunlight glinting off her wet golden hair.

Why wasn't I in the pool with her? Well, I was more interested in the redhead working the ice cream stand who'd given me a scoop of vanilla for free. Hormones, amiright? Sitting in my lounge chair with dark sunglasses on, I could check her out all I wanted, and no one was the wiser.

Then, sure enough, you heard this bone-rattling roar as the hydraulics kicked on. The waves began at last, big rolling peaks from way in the back that moved in a zigzag pattern toward the front. People hooted and hollered as the waves tossed them back and forth, back and forth. In the shallow end, Corinne shrieked with delight as she frolicked in the splashing water. "Johnny!" she shouted. "Look at me."

I gave her a thumbs up and turned my attention to the redhead again, lost in a creamy dreamworld of adolescent fantasies.

Next thing I knew there was horrible sound: *Ka-thunk!*

Someone screamed.

I jerked upright and looked out across the water. Near the back, the whitecaps were breaking. Only they weren't white. They were blood red.

It wasn't Corinne, thank God. She was still in the shallow end. I assumed the unimaginable had happened: a swimmer had been accidentally sucked into one of the propellers that created the waves, which should have been housed safely at the back of the pool.

That *is* what happened.

It wasn't an accident, though.

The waves became violent, churning and roiling. One by one, people were pulled under, their screams muffled by the relentless waves. Every time a body went under, I kept hearing it. *Ka-thunk. Ka-thunk. Ka-thunk.*

From somewhere deep underneath the pool, there was a thunderous, belching sound. The red tinge of the water crept toward the front.

I jumped up, scrambling across a sea of lounge chairs toward Corinne, who was struggling to move toward me in the surge.

I'd just made it to the edge of the sloping ramp that led into the pool. I was reaching out, ready to grab her, to haul her in—

Suddenly, a low rumble echoed through the park, and the ground began to tremble.

In the wall at the rear of the pool, two awful alien eyes appeared. Set deep within shadowy sockets, they glared out with a cold malevolence.

Impossibly, I knew I was looking at the eyes of a living alien creature. It trembled with anticipation in its disguised burrow. The wave pool itself was its mouth.

There was a cracking sound below. Under my feet, a fissure yawned open.

The sloping pool floor began to rise up. The people who were scrambling to safety now found themselves on a ramp that forced them away from me, back into the water. That's the last time I saw Corinne. She was sliding toward the churning, bloody froth, her angelic face twisted in a look of horror and confusion.

A strange humming noise filled the air and the pool itself began to transform. Sleek, metallic walls appeared on every side, forming a giant gleaming rectangle that trapped everyone inside.

My legs went weak as I watched the pool—now unmistakably a spacecraft—rise slowly from the ground and lift into the sky. It streaked off into the bright afternoon carrying my sister Corinne with it.

The thought of it—lying in wait all season until the busiest day of the year—to strike.

So, no thanks. I'll stay here on dry land if it's all the same to you.

I don't trust the water. You never know when it's hungry.

SHOW ME WHERE IT HURTS

In a stutter

Or your stupor

In a bitten fingernail

In your lies

Your bad advice

In your tendency to fail

A prescription

A compulsion

A regurgitated meal

In addictions

And afflictions

In the bruises you conceal

Your bleeding knees

Your STDs

In the lines upon your face

In your demands

Your fiendish plans

In the sins you can't erase

In your bad luck

Or a grudge fuck

In the tremble in your voice

In your scheming

And your screaming

In the lives that you destroy

In your wine glass

Or your wrecked ass

In your browser history

In aggression

And stagnation

In your endless cruelty

In delusion

And confusion

In all the truths you twist

Your violence

And negligence

In the scars upon your wrist

If your heart aches in misery

And life feels like a curse

Confess and on your pain I'll feast

Show me where it hurts

GOTCHA

The not-so-famous author was pacing near the window when the sidewalk gate clanged shut. His incredibly famous author wife waddled up the lane, dressed in dark clothes from shoes to hat, looking every bit 'the queen of modern horror'. Vanity Fair's term, not his. With shaking hands, he placed the box on the kitchen table. Inside his chest, his heart trembled like a caged bird.

"It's showtime," he muttered with a sneer.

She burst through the door like the miserable hurricane that she was, wearing the same dour expression she'd worn for the last thirty years. He forced a smile to his lips and ushered her to a seat at the table. "Happy birthday, my dear," he belted out with all the fake enthusiasm he could muster.

She glared at him spitefully and lifted the box's top. Her foul mood seemed to lift when she saw the magnificent cake inside. Chocolate Decadence with white buttercream frosting. Her favorite.

"Tell me all about the book signing," he said in as sugary a voice as he was able while making careful knife strokes through the cake's moist layers. "Were the people awful again?"

Her book sales outnumbered his a hundred to one, but her contempt for her fans had always been one of their secrets. She indulged him with a story about one "particularly horrendous" woman who had all but ruined her day. "She wanted me to autograph twenty books, all of which she'd brought from home." She shoveled a forkful of cake into the hole between her tremendous cheeks. "Can you believe it? The books were in a deplorable condition. Why, one was even bereft of its cover."

She paused for a moment, and something caught her eye. The top of the cake was shivering. Her eyes widened at first with curiosity and then with horror as several spindly legs poked through the frosting. Inside the confection, something was moving of its own accord—something alive. Suddenly, the cake collapsed upon itself. An enormous spider emerged from the dark spongy crater. It hauled itself out of its delicious prison like a zombie hand escaping a chocolate tomb.

Her fork clattered to the table when the thing reared back. It seemed furious to be there, and especially furious about the sticky goop coating its corpulent body. With a click of its jaws it scuttled toward her with terrifying speed, leaving an ugly brown smear on the tablecloth. At the edge of the table, the spider leapt toward her.

She jumped to her feet, and her chair fell back with a clatter. The spider plopped onto the linoleum, but by then the damage was done. She sucked in a breath to scream but it stopped abruptly. A look of confusion settled on her face. A guttural grunt sounded deep inside her throat. She grabbed the base of her neck with her hands crossed at the wrist—the universal sign for choking.

His voice dripped with sarcasm. "My dear, is something wrong?"

Her eyes bulged with panic. Crimson splotches exploded across her cheeks. She grabbed a nearby chair and slumped across it, centering the backrest directly beneath her ribcage. She heaved her body down once, twice, trying to clear the obstruction from her throat. It was no use. She dropped to her knees, then flopped onto her back. She wiggled around like a dying fish for a long moment before growing perfectly still.

He smiled down at her swollen, purple face.

"Gotcha," he said.

***

The spider was a Goliath Birdeater, one of the largest tarantulas in the world. She'd been a world-class arachnophobe for as long as he could remember. Throw in a recent case of heart disease, and, well... it was a time bomb waiting to happen. He'd hoped for a heart attack when she saw the spider. Choking had been an unexpected outcome, but one he'd happily accepted.

The arachnid had cost him a couple thousand dollars on the internet. Now that it had completed its mission, he didn't hesitate to squash it with a broom. Whack! He swept the mangled creature into the trash, along with the remnants of the ruined cake. In its stead he placed a second cake, an exact replica of the first, save for one minor detail—the new cake was missing the secret compartment in which he'd hidden the spider.

He cut himself a magnificent slice, but only allowed himself a single bite. He suffered from a touch of arrhythmia himself, so it was best to watch what he ate. Now that she was gone, he intended to enjoy his life for a long, long time to come. The rich chocolatey flavor satisfied him deeply. He sighed blissfully, before flushing the rest of the slice down the disposal. A moment later, he dialed for help.

"911," the voice on the phone said. "What's your emergency."

"My wife," he said, faking a desperate tone. "Please, hurry."

***

"Where were you when it happened?" the first officer asked, staring down at the cold body.

"The shower," he sobbed, surprised how the performance grew easier with every passing moment. "We were supposed to go out for dinner. I didn't even know she'd made it home." He threw himself against the wall and wailed in a pantomime of grief. "She was eating her," he paused for dramatic effect, "buh-buh-birthday cake without me!"

The second officer scrawled notes on a pad as he wandered through the mansion. He gawked in disbelief when he got to her study. The occult items she had gathered over the years lined every shelf—totems, candles, oils, talismans.

"Grim stuff," he said, flipping through a book on witchcraft.

"Research," the husband said. "It's what set her apart."

He refrained from mentioning the strange things he'd witnessed since she began dabbling in the dark arts. Like the eerie voices issuing from her locked study. The shallow grave full of slaughtered neighborhood pets in the yard. The night he'd woken to find her hovering above their bed.

In the kitchen, a coroner zipped up the body in a bag.

"Everything checks out," the second policeman explained. "But before we go—"

"Say no more." He handed the officers bags filled with pre-signed copies of her latest bestseller.

"Thank you," policeman #1 said.

"An honor," said policeman #2.

"I also included a copy of *my* latest novel, in case you're so inclined," he said with a smile. "Oh, and a few slices of cake for each of you. Please, enjoy."

***

At the funeral, security had to turn away many of her fans at the door. This was fine with him. The service was already a freakshow. Hundreds of weirdos huddled in pews in their gothic clothing. Their powdered faces cast a sickly sheen under the iridescent light.

He never understood how so many people could harbor an appetite for the themes she wrote about, all the violence, horror, and retribution. Their cold stares made him uncomfortable. More than once, they pointed in his direction, whispering to each other in hushed, secretive tones.

He decided they were jealous. She had chosen to spend her life with him, and they simply couldn't stand it.

By day's end, he'd forgotten them all.

His new life had begun.

***

A few nights later during a summer rainstorm he sat in his study working on a new novel. The inspiration was flowing, and words flew from his fingers with ease. While a wind picked up outside and thunder boomed in the distance, he typed out the final lines of the first chapter. He was deep in thought when the front gate clanged shut. Three sharp raps sounded on the entryway.

Who could it be? he thought angrily. How dare anyone disturb an artist such as he when he was immersed in his work! He expected no visitors, especially this late in the evening. He had half a mind to curse out whoever it was. In a rage, he crossed the room, and grabbed the door handle. Without thinking, he swung the door open wide.

In the pouring rain at the end of the doorstep stood a shadowy visitor. The scent of damp earth rattled his composure, and he felt his dinner rising in his throat. A flash of lightning revealed the knocker's identity—his dead wife! Her rotting eyes flashed with rage. Black beetles skittered across her sallow flesh. His blood ran cold when she lifted an accusatory finger in his direction. "Youuu!" she shrieked.

He stood unable to move, while his pulse pounded in his ears.

In one alarming motion, she charged toward him, her soggy shoes creaking against the doorstep.

Blinding fear assailed his body. He clutched at the sudden stabbing pain in his chest. No! he thought. His clenched teeth came down on the gristle of his tongue and the brawny tang of blood filled his mouth. Beneath him, his legs buckled, as he fell to the floor like a marionette cut from its strings. Slowly, he lifted his gaze to the nightmarish ghoul towering over him, before gasping out his final, painful breath.

"Gotcha," she croaked.

WE ′ RE ALL TRAPPED IN AN ETERNALLY RESPAWNING REALITY SIMULATION

Jayce recognized the man right away but couldn't remember his name. The man in the lobby smiled and nodded good morning. Jayce raised his thermos in a polite hello and continued on through the maze of office furniture. At his desk, he placed the thermos down next to the photo of his wife and took his seat. Why couldn't he remember the man's name?

Around him, coworkers settled into their chairs. Conference room doors closed. The printer chugged to life. He flicked the computer on, a dull whine churning in its belly. He would get to work in a moment, right after he remembered the man's name.

He blinked a few times, his eyes adjusting to the sterile fluorescent lights. The name was on the tip of his tongue. Roger? No, that didn't feel right. It was a punchy name, like Jack or Luke. The kind of name that belonged to a kid who might live next door, an all-American kid who would grow up to play football and date the prom queen.

Well, he would have to think about it later. His inbox was full, and his boss expected a report by the end of the day. Jayce eased his elbows onto the armrests. First, he would blast through his emails, make sure he wasn't missing something important. Then he would focus on the report. It would take most of the day to check the numbers before writing the report's conclusion. He lifted the thermos, took a sip of coffee. It was still hot, thanks to Linda. She'd handed him the thermos in the kitchen right before he'd headed to the car, same as every morning.

The bitter taste gathered at the back of his throat. Doug? No, that was still off. It was killing him that he couldn't remember the name. It was a name he should know. The man was a coworker, after all, not a stranger. They'd passed each other every morning for years. The two of them had lunched together many times, sharing stories about their families over cold sandwiches and limp pickle spears in the office cafeteria.

He slumped in the chair. He wasn't even forty, far too young to be having issues with his memory.

Was that what this was? He'd never had problems remembering things. Sure, sometimes he misplaced items around the house, like his phone. He'd work himself into a tizzy searching for it before Linda would ring his number. The phone would reveal itself, having slipped behind a cushion or been left in the bathroom. But that type of thing happened to everyone, didn't it?

Of all the mornings to be distracted. His report showed a way to save the company hundreds of thousands of dollars every quarter. If the report was well received, a promotion might be in his future, a salary increase, maybe even a private office. A better standing at work meant he'd be in a better position at home. He and Linda could use some good luck since the bank had denied their recent refinancing attempt.

He lifted his hands to his temples, worked his fingers into the tense tissue under his scalp. He tried to visualize the man's face, hoping the name would appear along with it. The man's features came to mind with no trouble at all: a broad face, brown eyes, auburn hair, slightly receding at the forehead. But the name did not emerge. He knew the name existed somewhere in his brain, complete and whole, if he could just find it. But right now, it felt like it was locked behind an iron door and buried under a ton of cement.

***

Lost in his thoughts, he was startled when a meeting invite dinged on his calendar. The meeting with his boss was set for 4 p.m. The subject line said Let's review the report. Jayce's heart sank when he glanced at the clock on his screen—he'd lost an hour and fifteen minutes thinking about the name. The situation was getting out of hand. If he didn't get the report going, there would be trouble later.

He leaned toward the screen and clicked open the report with his mouse. For a long moment, his eyes drifted across the page in front of him, his brain unable to recognize the numbers and words. The black markings looked like strange squiggles on a white background, like ancient hieroglyphs or some kind of alien language. He squeezed his eyes shut, suddenly aware of the tension in his shoulders, at the base of his neck, working its way into his skull.

He opened his eyes, stared again at the whiteness on the screen. His fingers hovered over the keyboard, but he could not think of what to write. He kept his body still, his face forward, feeling small and helpless in the ever-growing intensity of the fluorescent lights. The cursor flashed over and over again in silent mockery, almost daring him to fill the empty space with a letter, a number. Something meaningful.

Anything.

***

The minutes on the clock spilled along, one into the next. By 11:30 a.m., Jayce hadn't remembered the man's name.

He stared wide-eyed at his computer, a sense of unease coiling in his belly, his underarms damp with sweat. He opened the contacts folder in his mail program and searched through the names there. He searched one line at a time, over five hundred in all, looking for male names with one syllable. *Ambrose, Carl. Kuykendall, Bert. Montague, Luke.*

By the time he reached *Zapata, Gill*, he felt despondent. He bit the inside of his lip, his brain spinning in ever-frantic circles. In the back of his mind, it seemed like there was something else he needed to be doing, but he couldn't think of what it was. He picked up the thermos, took a sip of coffee, and was disappointed to find it had grown cold. He placed it back next to the photo, his gaze lingering on the woman's face in the frame. She was pretty, with wavy brunette hair, bright blue eyes, her lips curved into a coquettish smile. He felt like she was important, like he should know who she was, but he couldn't figure it out at the moment.

The air conditioner kicked on, circling dry air around the room. The printer coughed out sheets of paper. Jayce turned his head to look at the others in the room. Everyone appeared to be working fervently at their stations. He watched the efficiency in their movements, how their fingers glided on their keyboards like concert pianists, heard the helpful tones in their voices as they answered phone calls. He felt a sense of awe watching them, all of them so confident, so sure in what they were doing.

How unlike them he felt at that moment. What kind of worker was he if he couldn't remember one simple name? All he knew for certain was the light was hurting his eyes. He felt uncomfortable, the tension in his back and head fusing together in a throbbing wall of pain. He turned back to his computer, kept his fingers moving, lest his stillness call unwanted attention. He opened random documents with his mouse, all while trying to remember the man's name.

Was it Mike? Art? No. He dragged out the corners of the documents, resizing them into different squares, different sizes. Ben? Lou? He pecked random keystrokes on the keyboard and deleted them. Ralph? Scott? A sense of pressure grew in his bladder, all that coffee wanting to find its way out.

Names swirled around in his head, suspended there like some kind of alphabet soup, floating in a suspension of liquid white light. His body prickled with sweat. The light above him felt oppressive, heavy, as if it could crush him to death. He felt his chest tighten under all that weight, an invisible force threatening to squeeze the air from his lungs.

The name. He *knew* he knew it.

He could end all this if he could just remember it.

He stood up, his legs numb from sitting. He would find the man and ask him his name. He picked up the thermos, held it out in front of him, held it tightly with both hands like a prize that might slip away, no longer sure of where it came from, only that it imparted in him a small feeling of comfort and reminded him of something important, although he was no longer sure what the thermos held, or where it had come from, or what that important thing was. Slowly, jerkily, as if a marionette walking through a dream, he made his way through the office.

***

There, through the glass wall of a rear office, he saw the man he was looking for, the man who had smiled at him earlier. He was talking on his phone from behind a polished mahogany desk. Jayce stood outside the glass door, holding the thermos in front of him like a shield. He shifted on his feet from side to side, his bladder threatening to burst, the pain in his head now almost blinding. The man nodded for him to come in, waved for Jayce to take a seat.

The man finished his conversation, something about the second quarter and revenue and margins and projections. His voice was strange and loud. Jayce sat and waited, his eyes drifting from the wall of shiny certificates to the desk where a few framed photos sat next to a half-empty coffee mug.

The man brought his conversation to a conclusion and clicked the phone into its holder. He leaned forward in his chair, his hairy hands folded on the desk beneath him. "Mr. Miller," he said. "Better three hours too soon than a minute too late, eh? Is this about the report?"

The man knew *his* name. Jayce felt his mouth drop open, his lips struggling with the right words to say.

The man drummed his fingers on the desk. "Is something wrong?"

At last, a chance to end his agony. Jayce's head pounded. The office lights glared. His clenched hands gripped the thermos, the joints on his fingers now bone white. "Do—do I know you?"

The man's brow furrowed slightly, his brown eyes studying Jayce's features. Then, in one quick moment, his expression softened, and a smile exploded across his face. He slapped the desk, threw his weight back in his chair, and laughed a strange and loud laugh.

"Good one." The man wiped his eyes and then refolded his hands on the desk. "Had me going for a moment."

Jayce sat, unmoving. Mr. Miller, he thought. That's what he called me. Is that who I am? But who am I, really? Who is this man sitting in front of me?

The man spoke again, his tone somber. "Are you ill?" His nostrils flared slightly, and he glanced around the room. "By God, what's that smell?"

The man stood up and came around the desk. When he looked down at Jayce, he gasped loudly. "Christ Almighty, man! You've pissed yourself."

Jayce glanced down at the wet spot spreading on his trousers.

"Mr. Miller!" The man snapped his fingers in front of Jayce's face. "Do you need an ambulance?"

Jayce shook his head.

"Take the rest of the day off. Go home, Mr. Miller. You're not yourself today."

Jayce stood. The man shuffled him out and into the hallway. The door closed behind Jayce. Through the glass wall, he heard the man cursing under his breath.

Jayce held onto his thermos, his pants sticking to his legs, the wetness now cold against his flesh. Where was his desk? He was at work, yes, but what did it mean to work? Was this all a dream, a delusion, a figment of his imagination?

A woman sitting at a desk nearby noticed him first. Her eyes grew wide as she saw the wet spot on Jayce's pants. Like a domino falling, her look attracted another. Within seconds, everyone in the office was staring at Jayce as he stood there holding his thermos, a wet spot darkening the front of his pants.

Jayce blinked, trying to focus under the searing blindness of the lights. He saw no faces he recognized, only a roomful of inky black spots, each a window to a void that stretched deeper and deeper into infinity, pulling him into an emptiness he could not name and that he knew in his heart he would never be able to escape.

A VERY STABLE ZOMBIE

To believe the hype about the show, you'd think a man was about to walk on Mars. *Life Beyond Death* is what they called it. Mediocre title, but a killer tagline. "On October 31, the dead will rise." How could you not want to watch?

Seems like everyone tuned in that night. Some out of morbid curiosity. Others because they thought it would be a bust but wanted to gossip about it at work, like when Geraldo Rivera opened Al Capone's vault and found nothing but dirt and some empty rum bottles.

The businessman lay on a table wearing the clothes he'd been buried in, or so the narrator claimed. A skinny black man in a bone necklace and a thong danced around him, his naked torso shining with sweat. In the corner, a grim-faced organist pounded out a mournful dirge. Whole thing was pretty corny: oversaturated lighting like an amateur horror film, fake cobwebs looped in the corners, a papier-mâché moon hanging from the rafters. You've seen better sets on *Svengoolie*. At home, people either howled with laughter or shook their heads in boredom, already reaching for their remotes. Meme makers scrambled for their computers, ready to pounce on comedic gold.

Until those dead eyes fluttered open. Until the corpse sat up with a stiff jerk. Until his dry lips cracked apart, and a single, awful word twisted out into the world:

"Moneyyyy," groaned the dead-businessman-turned-reanimated-corpse.

It was the highest rated show in TV history.

The talking corpse was so popular, he took over the news cycle for a month. It didn't take long until the network gave him his own reality show. The premise was that you had to compete to be the corpse's best friend. Every week, he kicked off the person he disliked the most. "Die, loserrrr!" he'd growl, drenching the poor half-wit in a spray of rancid spittle. That show was something. The dead guy reeked so bad they had to film with the windows open, is what *TMZ* said. Every so often, one of his eyes would bulge out of its socket. A stagehand would have to rush out there to push it back in. Or they'd catch him chewing on his own tongue like it was a wad of bubble gum. He had a foul mouth, too, and he was mean; accusing contestants of being ugly, coughing all over the snack table, and even telling the sound guy, "Your mother eats crap in hell."

People ate it up.

Then, someone got the idea the corpse should run for president. What a joke, right?

It turned out to be the farthest thing from.

That election season was the craziest ever. The other politicians were defenseless in the face of the corpse's wild unpredictability. He steamrolled over them in debates. He called them dirty names. He bared his teeth and growled and spit and hissed. A senator from Florida was bit on the hand. Poor shmuck dropped out of the race before he even got to the hospital.

Somehow, this rotting, grinning ghoul became the party's nominee. And, in the most bizarre twist to ever hit the world of politics, managed to get himself elected.

The four years that followed were confusing for everyone. It was like a dark chasm had opened somewhere in the universe, one that threatened never to close. The dead president proved to be incompetent beyond imagining. He was prone to making impulsive decisions, like canceling Christmas and painting the White House black. He converted the Arlington National Cemetery into a huge condo and decorated it with enough gilded fountains to supply a small nation with water for a week. In public addresses, he was argumentative, contrary, hostile. He'd show up with a live python draped across his shoulders because ... why not? He spewed hateful rhetoric that stoked division amongst the citizens for hours on end, pausing only to swallow a live gerbil or to dislodge a maggot from his nostril. In world affairs, he cozied up to some of the country's biggest enemies while turning a cold, rotting shoulder to some of our staunchest, most dedicated allies.

What was stunning was how so many people embraced his insanity.

What was inspiring was how many people didn't.

When his four years dried up, the dead president was voted out of office. Of course, he wouldn't leave when they asked him to. "Squatters rights!" he snarled. "I'm a very stable zombie." He rallied his supporters to defend him; legions responded, sputtering up in rusty golf carts and motorized wheelchairs, cheap plastic Halloween skulls taped to the sides like the saddest apocalyptical army ever. Brandishing cattle prods and super soakers filled with pee, they scratched and bit, mimicking the undead antics of their leader, the air heavy with the smell of sweat and urine and the dying drone of "loser" fading like a funeral hymn. Dozens lost their dignity that day. At the center of it all, the corpse president cackled with glee.

Eventually, the local mall cops stepped in to disperse the mob. The dead president was thrown out of office, and a new president took over.

What happened to him after, you ask?

The network knew they had a problem on their hands, but damned if they weren't going to capitalize on it. They buried him under twenty tons of cement in a primetime special called Elegy: A Nation in Mourning.

Ever so slowly, things returned to normal.

Over time, the country looked back on that era as one of deep confusion. Some thought the world had been on the verge of collapse, while others insisted it all had been blown way out of proportion. No matter where they landed, though, everyone agreed on one thing: the dead president's term had been a big letdown, like when Y2K turned out not to be the end of the world, or that time Geraldo opened Capone's vault and found nothing but dirt and empty bottles.

The End?

IN THE CLUTCHES OF THE WRITING GODS

James Joyce. Virginia Woolf. David Foster Wallace. Literary giants like these don't simply happen, you know. They're *created*. By us. It's what we do, me and my husband. It's *all* we do.

No, these authors are not born with their gifts if that's what you thought. My husband Xander and I create them. Except Xander is pretty useless,s if you want to know the truth. So, basically it's just me. Doing all the work by myself. Day in, day out.

Quith's the name. At least it's what Xander calls me. Nobody else knows of our existence. I'm what humans might call a goddess. Technically, that would make Xander a god, but he's probably the lousiest excuse for one ever. Both of us decide who makes it in the literary community. You see, eons ago somebody—or something—put us here in our home up in the clouds where we monitor the world's writers for signs of greatness. We can pretty much see every word ever written from up here. Then, with our awesome powers, we help the ones we deem worthy become true artists in their fields. An extra push is often all it takes. It's an awesome job and an important responsibility.

And sweet jumping Jesus, is it ever boring.

Don't get me wrong. Every once in a blue moon comes along that rare writer who's pure of heart and blazing with an internal fire. I've mentioned a few already. When you see souls like that, it's an honor to help them. More than an honor, it's our duty. Or at least mine anyway. I just zap 'em with a healthy burst of inspiration and— boom!—they're on their way. Well, Xander mostly sits around scratching his balls. But me, I like to stay busy. When I see that spark of greatness on a budding new writer, everything comes alive. Those are the moments worth living for.

But lately, lemme tell ya, it's a lot of the same thing over and over again. The same worthless dreck from the same talentless pool of writers, poor deluded souls. If not for them, I'd have plenty of time to do whatever I wanted up here. But oh no! As long as they write, we have to monitor. Them's the rules.

You can't blame a gal for growing to hate it after a while.

This morning is a perfect example. I was sitting on my cloud, keeping an eye on humanity with my hawklike vision. The sun was shining just right, and I was feeling pretty amazing in my new leggings from Lululemon and my Hell's Angels jacket, with my pink mohawk fluttering lightly in the breeze. Down below, I'd just found a writer who interested me, when all of a sudden, I heard someone singing:

"Get up offa that thing, and dance 'til you feel better!"

Xander was awake. The cloud beneath me shook from his thunderous voice. From his James Brown impression and whiff of weed I caught, it was safe to say he was already high. He wore a studded leather collar around his neck and nothing else, which meant he'd woken up in a lusty mood. Just my freaking luck.

Worse, he was gyrating across the dais toward me.

If he was trying to turn me on, I had news for him. The sight of his bare jiggling flesh did nothing for me anymore, sexually. Besides, I had a job to do. I did my best to ignore him.

Until he reached under my t-shirt and gave one of my nipples a sudden, hard pinch.

Moving with dizzying speed, I bent his pinky finger back until bone snapped beneath skin.

"Gawdamn!" Xander recoiled in pain, the big baby. His celestial powers were already at work mending the injury. "What ya do that for?"

I yanked an unlit joint from behind his ear and ground it to bits beneath my leather boot. "Heads up. We've got a live one down there."

He sidled up beside me for a better view. "Oh, goody. Any talent?"

I couldn't tell yet. I needed a few more minutes to figure that out.

Her name was Beverly Davenport. Middle aged. Stringy red hair with a gray streak in it. Pretty average looking. She sat in her apartment, typing away on what she hoped would be her first published novel. She wasn't a great writer, and she knew it—a drawer full of rejection slips from uninterested publishers reminded her daily. But she could work all day and into the evening, so that counted for something. She was giving it all she had, which I knew from experience, would never be enough.

What can I say? I was looking to have a little fun.

"Ready to rock?" I asked Xander, popping up the collar on my jacket.

"Hells yeah," Xander said.

With the snap of a finger, a bolt shimmered down from the heavens, sizzling through rainclouds, and frying three unsuspecting pigeons before blasting through Beverly's ceiling and into the top of her head.

"Hot damn!" Xander said. "Love it when you do that."

I rolled my eyes. The lummox possessed the same power as me. He was just too goddam lazy to use it.

Same as always.

***

One moment, Beverly had been typing at her desk.

Then, an explosion.

She screamed and wet herself. Waves of raw talent coursed out of the lightning bolt and into her body, filling her with unbridled literary skills the likes of which only come along every few generations. When the transformation finally stopped, she blinked and looked around her room.

Alas, her senses were stronger than ever.

She sniffed the air and became aware of aromas which heretofore had escaped her, traces of pollen and chemicals and the stink of grease from last night's BLT sandwich. Where before she heard electricity humming in the walls, now the droning buzz of capitalism roared in her ears as it entangled humanity in its sinister web. In a speck of dust floating by, she now saw an entire universe unto itself, a dynamic superstructure composed of millions of molecules and atoms all pulsing and streaking around like tiny beams of light.

Unable to focus on any single image, Beverly's eyes rolled back in their sockets, and behold!—there were sentences back there, a swirling wonderland of complex and intricately constructed passages that would one day open minds and melt hearts. And so many stories! Everywhere she looked, she found magnificent plots filled with relevance and meaning, enough to finally make the masses bow down before her greatness.

She struggled to make sense of things. Part of her wanted to hide from the glaring brightness of this new reality. Another part wanted to capture the ideas on paper. But where to start? There were too many possibilities running around in her head, too many interesting situations and characters, all screeching for her attention like needy children.

So, dazed, drooling, befuddled, she fumbled for her desk organizer. Her fingers curled around the pencil she'd sharpened to a fine point only yesterday. With her other hand, she scrambled for a scrap to write on, blinded as she was could not find anything. Desperate to capture the thoughts before they escaped her, she lifted the pencil to her face, rested the tip for a moment against the bottom of her eye—and pressed it in.

The membrane popped. The nerves inside erupted in a chorus of agony that only she could hear. Warm jelly trickled down her face. No, not jelly. What was the name for the substance? She'd known it once. Had learned it back in grade school.

Ah, yes. The vitreous humor.

"Silly name for eye juice," she moaned.

She began to write. The pencil worked its way back and forth in the socket, turning the spongy matter of her brain into hamburger. Her body spasmed violently before spilling to the floor where she flopped around like a lazy gymnast, and then grew still.

Like that, Beverly was dead.

***

In the heavens, Xander howled with laughter.

I ran my fingers through my hair. Normally, I would've gotten a kick out of such a scene, but today it had left me feeling strangely tense. The struggle had ended too quickly. A good fight made the day go by faster, but that was people for you. The human mind could only take so much abuse before it unraveled. Maybe Beverly had just had a bad day.

So, with Xander hooting and snorting, I waved my powerful arms, rolling back time a few minutes on the planet below. When I was done, Beverly sat at her desk again, hearty and whole.

"Let's try a different tack," I said. With a wink of my eye, I dialed up Beverly's inner critic, which is a pesky hobgoblin for creativity as any artist can attest.

***

New Beverly opened her eyes slowly, her pupils contracting for the first time (but not really) to the afternoon light.

All seemed normal, she thought. She was in her apartment on a gorgeous morning, working away on her novel. A blank page waited on the screen, eager to be filled up with her brilliant musings.

She started to write. Paused.

She started again. Stopped.

The few words she'd written seemed bland and colorless. A five-year-old could have done better. She dragged the cursor across the screen, pressed delete.

Outside, the sprinkler started up, spraying water noisily onto the window. The sound woke the neighbor's dog from his afternoon nap, and he started to bark.

Why, she wondered, couldn't it be quiet when she was trying to work? Was that too much to ask from the universe? She hadn't asked for much in life, had she? Just a few things: a sturdy chair, an occasional sunny day, and a few quiet mornings with which to concentrate.

Gah! Why bother, anyway? Of all the things she could be doing with her time. Like needlepoint, for instance. Or gardening. Even sloughing off her skin with a cheese grater would be better than this.

Oh, but she was angry now. At the sprinkler, and at the dog. She was angry at everything she'd ever done that had led her to this moment. Who did she think she was, anyway, Sue-Fucking-Grafton?

Maybe some fresh air would help.

Outside, it was an impossibly bright day. Too much. The excessive light hurt her eyes and made things worse.

She paced the sidewalk, wondering how could she, a modest woman of modest intelligence, have let her life get to this point? Alone and unpopular, locking herself away for weeks at a time, attempting projects that felt like they'd never be finished. It was all too depressing. She felt her face tightening, tears gathering in the corners of her eyes.

A postman stopped to ask Beverly if she was okay.

"I'm fine!" she screeched, before collapsing on a bench to sob.

The postman pursed his lips. *Seriously,* he thought. *A grown woman, carrying on in public like that.*

***

"You showed her," Xander mumbled, only half-paying attention. He was wrist-deep in a bag of cheese doodles and flipping through a porno mag.

My heart sank. What was wrong with me today? Normally, manipulating writers was as fun as fun got, but today it just felt like work. What was the point, anyway? Hell, even Xander was past the point of caring.

I made a few gestures, erasing Beverly from existence.

Only to rebuild her.

With a few modifications.

This time, I made a Beverly who enjoyed sleeping late. A Beverly who liked to slip Kahlua into her morning coffee. A Beverly who spent hours in front of the TV crushing her imagination under an endless parade of reality stars and gadget salesmen.

Most importantly, I made a Beverly without literary aspirations.

This Beverly had no urge to write whatsoever. Unless you counted a few poems she wrote in 8th grade when she had a crush on Bobby Wilcox. Of course, that ambition was stamped out the day her history teacher snatched a poem out of her hand to read before the class: *Bobby, Bobby, with your brown hair / If you only knew how much I care.* She'd been the laughingstock of the school for months, and that had been the end of that.

My task complete, I glanced down to see what Beverly 3.0 was up to.

***

Why am I sitting at my desk? Beverly wondered. It was time to meet Randy for the carpool. She mustn't be late for her job at the office. She headed to her living room where she could watch for him near the window. A book of short stories sat on the coffee table. How had it gotten there? It wasn't hers, clearly; who had time to read in this day and age? Someone at work must have loaned it to her, but she couldn't remember who. Regardless, she picked it up. Opened it to a selection by O. Henry. Started to read to pass the time.

She liked the story so much, she read the whole thing.

Twice.

It was nice, that story. Like cake for the soul. A thought burbled up from somewhere deep inside: *How lovely it would be if I could write something like that someday. Something smart, thoughtful, and pretty.*

Then Randy was in the driveway, one fat arm jiggling out the window, the other blasting on the horn. She put the book down, was forgetting about it already. Off she went, to her ordinary job with her ordinary coworker, both of them perfectly content in their ordinary lives.

***

In the sky, the day was waning. Xander was snoring, dreaming of big-breasted goddesses, I'd almost bet. Well, who could blame him? Today had almost bored me into a coma, too.

Although...

It hadn't been too terrible, had it? To let Beverly have that moment of happiness? To see her, for one amazing instant, perfectly content in her little world.

Well, the morning would be here soon enough, bringing many more Beverlys to play with—an inexhaustible supply of writers, their heads filled with dreams and their hearts pinned to their sleeves. Xander was sleeping, big surprise, so I snatched a joint from behind his ear and fired it up. I took a deep toke, breathed it out slowly, and that's when I got the idea.

With a snap, I conjured up old Beverly's typewriter, loaded it with a piece of paper. Maybe it was just the weed, but I was thinking I had lots to say on the subject of writing. Wouldn't it be great to record my thoughts for posterity? I sat down looking at the white sheet in front of me, gave my knuckles a good crack and lifted my hands into position. I mean honestly, how hard could it be?

THE TOY VILLAGE

With a smile on her face and a clipboard under her arm, Sue Delaney shuffled down the street behind her neighbor Millie Pratt near the end of their weekly walk of the neighborhood. Visions of a nice cup of peppermint tea were dancing in Sue's mind when Millie suddenly stopped near the curb in front of #32 Juniper Street. Millie lifted her glasses from the chain around her neck, pushed them onto her nose and stared down. "What in God's name?" she said, the corner of her mouth twisting into a fishhook sneer.

Sue's smile faltered. Up until now, it had been her favorite kind of spring day. Sunny and warm, with nary a hint of trouble in sight. Now it looked like that tea would have to wait. She hurried over to Millie's side and looked down.

In a patch of dirt surrounding an ash tree near the curb, someone had built a tiny village using toys and knickknacks. A handful of neatly dressed elves with full red cheeks and hauntingly lifelike eyes huddled in front of a plastic cottage. Sitting on a stone, a fairy couple stared wistfully skyward, their feet immersed in a layer of blue pebbles resembling a pool. A family of gnomes huddled near a green door wedged between two gnarled roots. The entire village was outlined in an immaculate ring of white pebbles. Tiny pinwheels spun lazily in the breeze.

Sue's eyes drank in every cheerful detail. In all her days of living in Northlawn, she'd never seen anything like it. She lifted a hand to cover the grin on her face.

"There goes the neighborhood," a voice grumbled nearby. Dressed in his old brown cardigan, Bob Owens limped toward them, his cane clacking on the pavement. The three lived next door to one another, their houses pressed together like biscuits on a sheet pan;

Bob in the middle, and Sue and Millie on either side. Bob wrinkled his nose at the garden. "Saw it earlier this morning. Sorry I'm late, by the way."

"That war injury acting up?" Sue admired his dedication. Ten years her senior, it was a wonder he joined them at all.

"Getting old is for the birds," he said with a grimace.

Millie turned her gaze to the house at #32 Juniper Street. "Now that the Northlawn Action Committee is wholly present, shall we proceed?"

Letting out a small sigh, Sue trudged up the path behind Bob and Millie. She hated confrontations. A neighbor had to do something really bad to merit a note on her clipboard. Mostly, she was content simply walking with Millie and Bob, especially on days like today with the sunshine tickling her skin, a chorus of birds serenading from the treetops, and the scent of honeysuckle floating in the breeze. Still, someone had to hold the neighborhood to certain standards. That's why they'd banded together in the first place. Together, they stood united, a bulwark against any forces of disorder that threatened to knock their precious community out of balance.

Mrs. Hulaska had only been in the neighborhood for about a year. Sue didn't know much about her, except that she was a reclusive type with a foreign accent. She'd bought Fred Davenport's old house for a song, when his surviving family couldn't decide what else to do with it.

Already the yard had gone go to hell. Tall weeds tugged and clutched on the fabric of their pants. Nut grass grew thick and wild in the pathway cracks. Litter was everywhere: soda cans, Styrofoam cups, strips of newspaper and discarded plastic bags. From somewhere in the thicket of the lawn, a cat yowled.

As they approached the porch, they heard music blasting from inside. A female singer was wailing about something in another language. Sue couldn't quite put her fingers on the tongue; it was guttural with lots of harsh 'h' and 'k' sounds that made her think of someone hacking up a lung. Millie looked exasperated; Bob responded by rolling his eyes dramatically.

A clowder of cats lounged at the top of the steps and all but one scampered away at their approach—a large gray cat tomcat. It hunched its back and stared at them with intense, yellow eyes. Bob shook his cane, and the cat hissed before scampering off into the bushes.

The concrete porch was strewn with dirt, kibble and cigarette butts. A multitude of smelly feeding bowls were strewn about, all smeared with cat food and swarming with hungry flies. Overhead, the peeling paint was thick with dust and cobwebs. A stiff mop leaned against the door frame reeking of mildew.

"Awful," Bob said. A vein popped out along the side of his neck. "Ready?"

Mille nodded forcefully, and Sue sucked in a deep breath.

There was no answer when Bob knocked.

"She can't hear you," Millie said matter-of-factly.

Bob gruffly knocked again. This time the door rattled in its frame.

The music stopped. Heavy footsteps sounded inside. The door creaked open, but a security chain held it in place. A plume of pungent incense wafted out, and Mrs. Hulaska eyed them from the shadowy gloom.

For a moment, the only sound was her thick, wet breathing. It was the first time Sue laid eyes on her. A flimsy purple housecoat strained over her ample belly. Her dark hair was wiry, streaked with gray and pulled back into a tangled bun. An unfortunate mole bulged from of her chin like a fat dog tick. "*Jes?*" Mrs. Hulaska said.

Millie stepped forward, shoulders back, her chin jutting out. "How do you do? We are here as representatives of the Northlawn Action Committee. Do you have a moment to talk about your yard?"

A heavy crease crinkled Mrs. Hulaska's forehead. "What ees wrong with jard?" Her accent was thick and throaty, like the singer they'd just heard. European. Possibly Italian or Hungarian. Sue stole a look into the living room. A scuffed coffee table was covered in gems and crystals next to a spread of tarot cards.

"Now, Northlawn has a reputation to uphold," Millie said.

Cringing at Millie's tone, Sue stepped forward. "Why, just last year we were voted Best Neighborhood in the *Dallas Tribune*."

Millie's lips pressed together in an attempt at a smile. "Awards like this don't happen by chance," she said more to Sue than anyone else. She turned back to Mrs. Hulaska. "It's the combined efforts of our neighbors that make this place such a nice place to live. Now, if we all pull together—"

"Oh, posh," Bob blurted out, his upper lip quivering. "Look, clean up your yard already, especially those stupid toys. And while you're at it, do you need so many goddamn cats?"

The color of Mrs. Hulaska's cheeks went from olive to bright red. She blinked rapidly like her eyes had taken on dust. "Please," she said, retreating back into the shadows. "Leave me."

"Mrs. Hulaska," Millie said, in a louder tone. "We're asking you nicely."

"If you don't like it, we'll be happy to get the city involved," Bob said.

"Bob!" Millie said.

The door banged shut. The music started again, louder than before. Bob's cane clicked as he descended the steps, with Millie following close behind.

Sue came last down the stairs. "That did not go well."

"What did you expect from that GYPSY?" Bob said, shouting the final word. Just as he reached the bottom step, a mass of fur sprang at him from the bushes. Before Bob could react, the large gray tomcat wrapped itself around his ankle. It spat and clawed and hissed and buried its fangs into the meat on the back of his good leg.

"Hell!" Bob lifted his cane and gave the cat a good couple of whacks. The cat scrambled away before stopping to glare at Bob.

"Oh, dear," Millie said, rolling up Bob's trousers. The puncture wounds were deep and bloody, and the skin there was already swollen.

Sue tried to drape Bob's arm around her shoulder, but he shrugged her away. "Let's get home," she said. "I'll drive you to a doctor."

"That's the last straw," he said through clenched teeth.

***

Bob received a couple of shots in his rump and a round of antibiotics for the cat bite. By the next walkabout, he appeared to have recovered nicely. He was in good spirits, too, and unusually chatty—until they passed in front of #32 Juniper Lane. Clearly disgusted, he sauntered across the street while Millie and Sue discussed the toy village.

"The nerve!" Millie said.

Sue stooped over to get a better look. "It's still here?"

Mrs. Hulaska—dressed in her housecoat—bound from her front door, screaming at them. She clutched a bundle of rags against her chest.

"Uh oh," Sue said, when Mrs. Hulaska started down the stairs.

Sue couldn't understand the words being hurled in their direction, but it was impossible not to read Mrs. Hulaska's state of mind. Her jowls shook with every lumbering step. Spittle flew from her mouth.

The bundle the woman carried wasn't rags at all. It was the gray cat that had attacked Bob. Today it was far less fearsome—it appeared to be quite dead. Its fur was matted and greasy, it's body stiff with rigor mortis.

"My Sinfi!" Mrs. Hulaska shrieked as she headed toward Bob. She held the dead cat out toward him like an offering. "Jew!" she shouted. "Jew keel heem! Jew poison heem!"

"Please," Sue said, stepping between them. "Calm down."

"Calm down?" Mrs. Hulaska shouted. "*Calm down?*" Her lips curled back to reveal her clenched yellow teeth. She hurled a new volley of strange words at them. Then holding the cat to her body with one hand, she made a circular motion around her heart, and the center of her forehead. She spat into the dirt and smeared the glob under the heel of her slippers.

"Okay, that feels threatening," Sue said.

"Let's get out of here," Bob said.

As they retreated, Mrs. Hulaska nestled the dead cat against her bosom and rocked it back and forth like a baby. "Sinfi," she moaned.

The three of them walked away in silence.

"If I didn't know better," Sue said to Bob, "I'd say she just laid a curse on you."

"The nerve," Millie said. "To insinuate that you would do something so awful."

Bob was silent, except for the cane. *Click, clack.*

"Bob," Sue said. "Tell me you didn't."

"This used to be a great place to live," he said.

Sue paused a moment, watching Millie and Bob walking away. If Bob had poisoned the cat, then he had gone too far. They were supposed to be helping the neighborhood, not getting revenge on people. *Mrs. Hulaska is atrocious, but she didn't deserve that. Should I say something?* she wondered.

In the end, she kept silent. Picking up the pace, she joined them again on the street. In the upper branches of a nearby elm tree, a starling squawked out an alarm call then scudded out into the calm blue sky.

*****

That night, Sue dreamed of a giant cat-god. It sat on its haunches on a large, gilded throne. In front of the entity, several globes were arranged on a stone table. The cat-god beckoned for Sue to approach. Shivering and fearful, she made her way across the cavernous hall. As she got closer, she could see that what she mistook for globes were actually replicas of Earth. The cat roared. It picked up a globe. With the slash of a mighty paw, it sliced off a hunk of land. This piece, the cat-god smashed into one of the other globes. It did this repeatedly with growing intensity, until Sue felt afraid. Her dream-self whimpered. The cat took it as a threat, hissing and lunging over the table toward her.

Sue woke up in her room, her heart thumping in her chest. Her phone was ringing.

"Ready for patrol?" Millie's voice said brightly through the phone.

"Wait, is that today?" Sue rubbed her eyes, feeling groggy and confused. Hadn't they just patrolled yesterday?

"Every week, like clockwork," Millie said. "Meet you out front in twenty minutes, sleepyhead."

Sue sat up for a moment, hoping to clear her head. She'd had an awful dream; but already it was gone. Why couldn't she remember it? When she tried, an awful feeling came over her. She readied for her day the best she could, struggling to put it all out of her mind.

Once she was dressed, she opened the front door—but something made her pause. When she looked out at Millie's house across the lawn, she felt woozy. Something was out of place, but what? For some reason, she had expected Millie's house to be two lots over. But no. It was right next door as plain as the nose on her face, a well-kempt Cape Cod with a blue door. It was right where it had always been. Wasn't it?

"Get a grip, woman," she said before heading down the sidewalk to where Millie was waiting.

Keeping pace today was an effort. Millie's walk was plucky and brisk, and Sue's body felt like it was full of lead. Was she getting ill? Maybe she was working too hard. Spring was always a busy time of year in the neighborhood, with all the requisite outdoor activities like gardening and Easter. There was lots to keep an eye on. Of course, she and Millie had known the committee would be a lot of work when they'd formed it years ago.

"Ever think we should add another member?" Sue asked.

"Heavens no," Millie said. "I like that it's just us. Like the saying goes: 'Too many cooks spoil the broth.'"

"Right," Sue said. They stopped in front of the toy village.

"Oh, brother," Millie said.

Sue remembered the village being smaller, maybe five feet in diameter. Now it was twice as big. Again, that strange sensation niggled at her, an undeniable feeling that something was off.

Millie waved a hand in front of Sue's face. "Mission control to Sue," Millie said. "Have you heard a word I've said?"

Sue blinked and turned her attention back to Millie. "Sorry. What?"

Millie glared at the toy village. "What do you think of the new addition?"

A new character had appeared. The wizard-like figure had gray, thinning hair, wore a brown cardigan and was propping himself up on a walking stick.

"Interesting," Sue said.

Mille crossed her arms in front of her chest. "Since that hag is in no hurry to clean up this mess, maybe we should give the toys names. What should we call the new guy?"

A name flashed into Sue's head suddenly and forcefully. Without hesitation, she said: "Oh, he's definitely a Bob."

***

They met at Millie's house the next evening for their monthly planning session, which started promptly at 5 p.m. At 6:00 p.m., Millie opened a bottle of wine. They chatted and drank and nibbled on cheese. Soon, the meeting took a backseat to gossip and giggling. When Sue looked at her watch again it was almost 9 p.m.

"Goodness." Sue tried not so slur her words. "It's late"

Millie got up from her sofa and emptied the bottle into her glass. "You can't go," she said, "not until we figure out who wins Yard of the Month." She released the elastic from the bun on her hair.

Sue thought her gray hair looked quite pretty, swinging loosely around her shoulders. She swirled the remainder of chardonnay in her glass. Her cheeks were flushed and warm. "Going to be hard to top the Applegates," she said. "That new fountain is the bee's knees. But Randy Shit-kowsky," she paused to chuckle, "I mean *Shi*-kowsky. Goodness, I'm tipsy. He's really stepped it up. Did you see the new azalea bed?" She tipped her glass to finish the last sip.

Millie's eyes flashed. "We should give it to Mrs. Hulaska."

The idea was so preposterous, Sue snorted, and chardonnay went down the wrong pipe. She doubled over in her chair, wracked in a spasm of coughing and laughter. "That's hilarious," she said in between gasps of air.

Millie made her way across the room. "Let's do it." She took Sue's hand and led her to the front door.

They stepped out into the dark. Quietly, they padded through the neighborhood, clinging to the shadows like a pair of burglars. Sue felt giddy and strangely excited. She hadn't done anything sneaky like this since childhood when she'd creep around throwing eggs at houses with her friends.

They stopped at the end of the Applegate's driveway. The lights in the house were off. Vernon Applegate worked early in the mornings; he was probably already asleep. In the middle of the lawn, the coveted Yard of the Month sign stood, a cheap sign made of poster board on top of a flimsy wire frame. Millie jostled it out of the dirt, while Sue waited under the shadows of an oak tree.

A few minutes later they stood in front of Mrs. Hulaska's house. "Here goes nothing," Millie whispered. She tiptoed past the toy village and into the lawn. With a defiant smirk on her face, she pressed the metal frame into position. Amid the tangled lawn and the strewn bits of trash, the sign looked ironic, ridiculous.

Back on Millie's sofa, the pair released all the laughter they'd been holding in. They howled and they wheezed and they slapped their thighs until they'd gotten it all out. When it was over, Sue wiped a few stray tears from her cheeks. When was the last time she'd let loose with such wild abandon?

Too long, she decided. Way too long.

***

The next morning Sue awakened with a banging headache. "Never again," she said as she as steadied herself down the hallway. In the kitchen, she gulped down two aspirin and made some hot tea. She had just settled into her favorite chair with a cold compress on her head when a new type of banging started. It was coming from outside, accompanied by the sound of someone shouting. Sue hurried to the window. Mrs. Hulaska stood on Millie's front porch. She was banging the Yard of the Month sign against Millie's door.

"Oh no," she said, remembering the events of the previous night.

She rang Millie's number. Millie answered, breathless and afraid. "Mrs. Hulaska's here! And she's furious."

"Tell me about it," Sue said, peering from behind the curtain.

"She knows!"

"Keep it together, Millie. It could have been anyone. There are lots of kids in this neighborhood."

The banging got louder. "Should I call the police?"

"Let me talk to her first," Sue said.

A moment later, Sue made her way over to Millie's house. Mrs. Hulaska was beating on the door, oblivious to anything but her rage. The sign was pulverized. "Coward!" Mrs. Hulaska shouted. "Jew open thees door!"

Sue nervously cleared her throat. "Mrs. Hulaska."

Mrs. Hulaska whirled around, her nostrils flaring. "Jew! Jew defend her?"

"I came to apologize," Sue said. "It was a stupid prank."

Mrs. Hulaska shook what was left of the frame in the air like a club. "Jew confess, then? Both of jew do thees to me?" She hurled the broken frame into the yard and stomped down the steps.

The front door opened, and Millie stepped out. "Leave her alone," she said. "It was my idea."

Mrs. Hulaska stopped and turned her wrath toward Millie. Her face was hard and grim. She fixed her gaze on Millie for a long and uncomfortable moment. Then the scowl on her face twisted into a grin. A chuckle rumbled deep inside her chest and burst out of her mouth like a ruptured sewage pipe. She turned and waddled down the sidewalk, leaving them to wonder what had happened.

"Thank you," Millie said finally in a weak, thin voice. She looked pale, like she might throw up. "Please come in. I'll put on some coffee."

They sat quietly in Millie's kitchen. The percolator sputtered and the aroma of coffee slowly filled the room. It was a long time before either of them could stop shaking.

***

Another night, another terrible dream.

This time, the dream involved a close friend. Sue didn't know her name, only that they had been friends for a long time. The two were walking down a street, when a dark thundercloud appeared. It started to rain hard. As the raindrops pelted them, Sue took the friend by the hand to lead them to shelter. The friend would not move; she stood stiff and immobile, staring straight ahead. When Sue looked down at the friend's hand, she realized the woman was made of salt.

To Sue's horror, the woman melted away, her flesh, bone and muscle dissolving into a frothy pinkish sludge that flowed away into a gutter.

Sue bolted upright in bed, screaming. The dream faded away, but she felt close to panic, her body covered in a layer of sweat. Nothing appeared out of order in her bedroom. Over here was her dresser, same as always. Over there, the tiffany lamp that once belonged to her mother. Everything was as it was supposed to be.

Why hadn't she gotten up at 5:30 a.m. like always? It was late—already 7 a.m. She slumped out of bed, already feeling lousy about herself. There was so much to do today. As the only member of the Northlawn Action Watch, she had to stay on top of her duties. It was up to her to keep the neighborhood running smoothly.

It ended up being one of those mornings. She scalded herself with hot water in the shower. Stubbed her toe on the dresser. Burned her morning toast. By the time she stormed out the door with her clipboard, she was in a real mood. *Is it time me to take on a partner to share in the duties?* Probably not, she decided. *Too many cooks always spoiled the broth.*

The clipboard seemed to fill itself that day. Several yards had been negligent in their mowing obligations. The Smith's rottweiler was off leash again, chasing squirrels through a neighbor's yard. The trim on the Patterson's house needed touching up, what were they raised in a barn?

Then there was the travesty at #32 Juniper Lane.

Mrs. Hulaska's toy village was out of control. How could Sue ever have thought it was cute? The tacky plastic houses. Those ridiculous figurines with their garish costumes. The spooky grins on their stupid little faces. It was getting bigger, too, having expanded to about a fifth of Mrs. Hulaska's lawn. There was a new character today that hadn't been there yesterday. A little peasant woman. She was old, her gray hair up in a bun, glasses dangling from a chain around her neck.

Why, just looking at the mess made Sue's blood boil. It was so vulgar and tacky. It didn't belong here in Northlawn. And since nobody else was going to do anything about it, Sue had to do something about it herself.

She stalked up the sidewalk, her temples throbbing. The screen door was open, but the house inside was dark. She banged on the door. "Mrs. Hulaska!" she shouted. "Where are you?"

Sue pressed her face to the screen and looked in. Everything was still. As her eyes adjusted to the light, she saw a bulky figure sitting on the couch, shrouded in darkness.

"There you are! I know you see me," Sue said. "This trashy shit in your yard has got to go! Do you hear me?"

Two pinpricks of green light flickered where Mrs. Hulaska's eyes would be. The shape on the couch did not move.

"Go back to your country, you piece of shit!" Sue screamed through the door. "We don't want your kind here!"

When she got home later, her heart was still pounding. She opened a bottle of wine to help her calm down. She drank the first glass quickly, and had another, and before she could stop, she'd finished the whole bottle. Then she sat on the couch and cried for a long time. *Why can't everybody do what they're supposed to?* she wondered. Eventually, exhaustion got the best of her. She curled up into bed, closed her eyes, and slept.

***

Sunlight was cracking like an egg over the horizon, drenching the neighborhood in a glow of warm golden sunlight. Amelia and Benny Gables, a pair of wide-eyed dreamers in their late twenties, pushed a stroller that cradled their pink bundle of joy, little Megan. The couple was glad they'd chosen Northlawn to settle down in. The houses, with their brightly colored flowerbeds and well-manicured lawn, exuded a welcoming charm that made them feel instantly at home.

In front of #32 Juniper Street, Benny stopped pushing the stroller. "What in the seven rings of hell is this?"

"It's a hot mess, is what it is," Amelia said, her eyes narrowing with displeasure. Together, they stared down at the toy village.

Benny squeezed his hands into fists. The eyesore stretched out over a third of the lawn. Amelia's eyes drifted over the different figurines but were drawn back to one in particular. It was a little toy fairy. She was old and wrinkly, but a fairy nevertheless, with silky wings on her back and flowers in her silver hair. The fairy gazed out at the village with a look of fondness on her face. It was a look that seemed to appreciate the quaintness of the village, where everything had its place, where it was peaceful every day and she got to hang out with friends she'd known for years.

"Not in my neighborhood," Benny said.

"What are you going to do?"

"Wait here." He started up the path to the house. Amelia grabbed the stroller's handles and little Megan cooed as her father neared the porch.

From somewhere in the thicket of the yard, a cat yowled.

CICATRIX

Peeping through a crack in the heavy brown curtains she looked out past her own pale reflection to see the other children in the street, all of them laughing and running and playing in their bright jumpers and wool trousers, sunlight shimmering off their finely combed tresses, and she thought she loved them, she loved them all, and she made up stories about who they were, like that one is named Ricky and he will grow up to be a farmer, and she over there is Jackie who will become a movie star but then die too young from a hole in her heart, and oh, she wanted to be just like them. She said it to her daddy, or tried to, her clumsy mouth struggling to form words over her fat tongue and bulging teeth, but he yanked her from the window and shook his big hairy finger in her face and told her no no no and she thought he was a good daddy even though he kept her inside the house like a prisoner with locks on all the doors and windows all day all year all her life like when he had to go to work sometimes and to the grocery to buy their food and the only time she felt sun on her skin was on Christmas morning. That's when everybody in the village was opening gifts and eating pheasants and jelly and singing songs about Harold the angel, so he snuck her into his rickety pickup truck and drove her to the pond at the edge of the woods where she could enjoy the outdoors for a while, but only if she would hide her face under a sheet, because they wouldn't understand if they saw her, he said, they never ever would, and on those days sometimes it was cold and sometimes it was snowing but every once in a while there would be sunshine and she liked those days best of all, the feeling of warmth like butterflies on her skin and her face and her hands. Yes, she loved her daddy and the only time he ever whipped her was when he caught her trying to sneak out that one time and fast went the branch whizzing through the air, pain exploding on her buttocks, tears streaming from his eyes as he told her he loved her, his sweet and only baby girl, and that this was for her own good, and she believed him, she did, because she knew she was different when she looked in his shaving mirror. It was something called *genetics* he told her, just confusion in the blood, and there was nothing she could do about it never ever never, and he dabbed at her wet eyes while her claw-like hands probed her face and her bulging brows and her bald head, her eyes watching from sunken sockets and the slits of her nostrils bubbling with snot, and her mouth gaping, an almost perfect circle of darkness from which extended her long pointed teeth, all of her features so different from the other children, but on the inside she was just a girl. So she stayed inside and she hid and she hid all through the days and the months and the years that piled up one after another like a crashed train with only her daddy and the house and her dolls to play with, and she was happy she thought, because her daddy kept her company and kept her tummy full and on Sundays they would play church together, she in her favorite black dress, spraying herself with jessamine until she smelled like a queen, and they would talk about the scriptures and Jesus and the wonders of the Bible, and she asked why don't miracles happen anymore daddy? and he told her, they will someday, that good things would come to her if she only believed, and so she did, she believed, in Jesus and the pearly gates and all that holy stuff because a better day was coming for her, she just knew it in her little girl bones. So what a shock it was one day when her daddy slumped over the table at dinner, his hand clutching at his chest and his face three shades of blue, and when he stopped breathing she shook him and she called for him daddy daddy daddy but he would not stir and so she rubbed his chest and she sang to him, but the next morning he still would not move so she combed his hair and sat next to him on the floor, and she did this for days until the food ran out and a big stink filled the house and there wasn't enough jessamine spray in the world to get rid of it. In the end she listened to the thrumming in her heart and she wiggled into her black dress, the taffeta rustling like paper, the tulle scratching at her legs like burweed, and she held her breath and with quivering hands she unhooked the keys from daddy's belt, and the lock on the door clinked softly and the door creaked open, and she stepped off the porch and into the sepia-colored yard all covered with dust and trash and dead patches of grass, and in a few more feet she was out of the shadows and out of the yard and bathing in golden sunlight, and it rained down on her and washed over her and it felt so good, it felt like all the angels in heaven singing all at once, and then the sounds of the children in the street calling and shouting and running were like a beacon to her and she thought she must join them, but she'd make a better impression if she smiled because everyone loves a smiler, so she tilted her neck back and lifted her chin up and she pulled her thin lips back past her enormous teeth and gave them the biggest smile she had, the one she'd been saving for years and years, and it felt wonderful, like Jesus at the resurrection, like all the miracles in the Bible coming to pass all at once, because this was her second chance at life, her chance to start again, so she could hardly believe her ears when the first of the children screamed...

SPINELESS

Tildy barked and stood by the door in that way that told him she needed to pee. Willis glanced at the clock and sighed. It was later than he would have liked. The evening's western had drawn him in. He'd always loved movies about brave heroes winning against impossible odds. But who was he to deny the biological needs of his precious Maltese? The quicker he took her out to do her business, the quicker the two of them could climb into bed. His old bones creaked as he crawled out of the recliner. With a click, he secured the leash onto the dog's beaded silver collar, and together, they slowly made their way to the park.

Willis fidgeted nervously in the cool air, partly from the chill and partly from his social anxiety, which always made him edgy in public. People were to be avoided. They either felt sorry because you were old, or they wanted to take advantage of you. Either way, he had no time for it. At least tonight, the park seemed pretty empty. Regardless, Willis gripped the leash tightly, keeping his pace steady and his eyes down. Tildy was sniffing curiously at the edge of the sidewalk when a muffled cry interrupted the quiet. Willis picked the dog up and held her tightly to his chest. When he heard a second cry, nosiness got the better of him, and he crept to the top of the hill to see what the matter was.

He quickly wished he hadn't.

An assault, in progress. A street thug crouched over an old woman. A torn burlap bag lay at her feet, and her belongings spilled out in every direction. In the thug's hand, a knife gleamed in the light of a nearby lamp.

Willis sucked in a breath. The woman was one of the beggars that occupied the park. He'd seen her often, squatting in the dirt near the sidewalk with her grubby outstretched hands, a powerful odor wafting from the folds of her tattered rags. He wasn't opposed to giving handout to the needy from time to time, but this woman—there was something off about her, something dangerous. The archaic symbols she drew in the sidewalk with chalk. The strange utterances that spewed from her warty lips. The bucket of dirty cloth dolls she carried, metal pins mashed cruelly into their eyes, their hearts.

The woman noticed Willis. The thug had clamped his hand over her mouth, but her bulging eyes spoke volumes. She wanted him to help. But what could he do? He was a retired librarian, not a hero.

The thug's eyes followed the woman's gaze. When he saw Willis, a grin stretched across his thin lips. He released his hold over the woman's mouth and ran a finger across his throat. Willis shrank into the shadows.

The woman struggled against her captor. She kicked and spat but the thug quickly pinned her down again. She fixed her eyes on Willis once more. "Spineless coward," she screamed. "Help me!"

The knife arced down. Willis turned away. He clutched the dog to his chest and prayed he wasn't followed and didn't stop moving until he had reached his apartment.

With shaking hands, he double bolted the door and poured a tumbler of brandy. He gulped the drink down and stared at the phone on his desk. Once his nerves settled, he would call the police. But what good would it do? The thug would be gone by then. Worse, he would know Willis had reported him.

Willis contemplated this predicament. Anytime he left his apartment, he would have to look over his shoulder. He imagined the thug lurking behind every corner, crouching behind every bush. The woman had been old, but she hadn't been small. If the thug could take her down, what could he do to Willis? Or Tildy? In the end, Willis chose to do nothing. It wasn't his responsibility. The city hungered, and the city fed.

He guzzled down another three fingers of brandy. Somewhere after one o'clock he undressed and stumbled off to bed.

***

When he woke later, it was because of Tildy. A series of shrill barks told him she was at the door. He lay on his back and blinked in the harsh daylight. From the way the light played across his tiny bedroom, he could tell it was late afternoon. He had lost an entire day. What was wrong with him? Why did he feel so strange?

Then he remembered the brandy and what had made him drink it. A shudder passed through his body. Hopefully, a jogger would have happened across the crime scene by now. The police would already have been called, the coroner dispatched to haul off the body. Willis couldn't bear thinking about it. Maybe he would walk Tildy in the opposite direction today. Or at the very least, take a peek at where the attack had occurred, but from a safe distance.

Get up, old man, he thought. He tried to sit up, but nothing happened. His arms and legs lay useless at his side. It was like his brain was sending the proper signals, but his limbs were ignoring them.

He was unable to move.

Was he paralyzed? Perhaps he'd had a stroke in his sleep. Yes, that was it. The trauma of what he had seen had been too much for his senses. Or maybe he was finally paying the price for years of unhealthy living. Either of those events was possible.

But *was* it a stroke? Strokes affected the brain, nd he was thinking clearly enough. Maybe it was something else. He considered several medical possibilities. Maybe the brandy had gone toxic. Or he had developed the palsy. *Take it easy*, he thought. *Getting worked up won't do you any good.* He opened his mouth to take in a few deep breaths. The act took considerable effort. A gurgle sounded from deep inside his chest as he struggled to take in air.

At the door, Tildy barked louder.

His precious little dog. What would become of her if he was ill? He'd raised her since she was just a pup, and she depended on him for everything. Tildy was more than a dog. She was his confidante. His best friend. He avoided relationships with other people, but he could always count on his loyal girl for companionship. She was his whole world. He owed it to her to try again.

Daddy's coming, sweetheart, he thought. He took in a deep breath, exhaled, and strained once again to lift upright. Nothing. On the third exhale, however, there was movement. His body shifted. Not much, maybe an inch. Enough to give him hope. With renewed vigor, he swallowed air until his lungs swelled, and then strained to move as the air left his chest. Slowly, he managed to rock his body back and forth in ever-increasing undulations. In one final push, he hurled himself off the bed. His arms and legs flailed around his body like flabby rubber bands as he fell, but he had no time to consider this startling fact because next thing he knew he was hitting the wood floor hard with a sickening plop.

The intense pain blinded him for a moment. When the spots in his eyes slowly cleared, he found he had landed in front of the full-length mirror.

But what was he seeing? A heap of naked flesh lay crumpled on the floor like an empty plastic bag. At the bottom of the pile, his face was visible, sunken in and folded from the weight of the body that crushed it. His eyes gazed out in horror as he took in the rest of his strange configuration. His limbs, slack and rubbery, spilled around him at uncommon angles. The blubbery mass of his torso made up the bulk of the pile. Above that, the shock of gray, unruly hair that marked his pubis. His flaccid penis dangled sadly to one side like an animal's snout. Yawning open at the top like an unblinking eye was the puckered opening of his anus.

He struggled to stand up, to move at all, but couldn't. His body no longer possessed a skeleton.

It was then that he remembered the words of the beggar woman in the park.

He tried to scream but all that came out was a dull, mournful moan.

***

The hours passed slowly. There was nothing he could do but lie on the floor and watch as the daylight faded into night. Sometime in the darkness Tildy drained her bowl of water and then went scouting for food. Her plastic dish made a scraping sound when she nudged it across the floor. An hour or two later—it was impossible to tell time— she began to bark. He hoped someone would hear and come to investigate, but he doubted it would happen. He'd chosen the apartment at the end of a long hall specifically because of his noisy dog. No one would hear her now. Or even care. He'd made his desire for privacy known, and the other residents gave him a wide berth.

Tildy barked for a few moments and stopped. The next thing he heard was her urinating on the living room floor.

In the reflection of the mirror, he could see the bolted living room door in the next room. How that lock taunted him. There was nothing he could do to reach it.

***

By the third day the apartment stank of their waste. Misery consumed Willis' every waking moment. But at least Tildy had stopped barking and whimpering finally. For the last few hours, she had been lying nearby, studying him with her curious eyes. Every so often she let out a whine that transformed into a low, throaty growl. The poor thing. She hadn't had food or water in several days. Was it his imagination, or were the bones of her ribcage starting to show through the skin?

Strangely, the frustration of his cramped, unnatural position overrode his own needs. Every waking hour filled him with hopelessness and despair. He didn't hunger. He knew he could go several days without food or water, but what about the dog?

It made him remember an event from his childhood. One winter, a stray dog had slipped into his father's barn, unaware to anyone in the family. His father had locked the dog inside and then driven the family to visit relatives. When they returned after their week away, his father opened the barn and discovered their guest. The dog was exhausted but alive. She had been pregnant. They didn't learn this immediately, however. There were no squealing pups anywhere to be found, no warm bodies sucking milk from her teats. The family realized it only when they examined the scattered piles of her stool. The bloody lumps were filled with tiny, splintered bones. As long as Willis lived, he would never forget gazing down at all those bits of skull and feet. The dog had felt no remorse for what she had done. She had hungered, and she had fed.

Tildy whimpered. She rose to her feet and crossed the room. The wet snout of her nose pressed into the flesh of Willis' back. She sniffed there a little, moved toward his neck, sniffed again. Her rough, sloppy tongue found his face and she began to lick. The sensation was a tonic after so many days without physical contact. Willis wept as his heart swelled with love.

By the time she took her first nibble, it was almost a mercy.

THE TROUBLE WITH GOBLINS

"What should we do with the body?" the goblin Sulphur said, releasing her hold on the victim's neck. She was panting with excitement from the kill, her scaly chest heaving, fresh blood congealing under her long, jagged nails. The man in the scarlet cloak flopped to the stone floor with a sickening whump.

The last few minutes had been quite confusing. One moment she and her sisters had been locked away in their limbo-like prison, where they'd spent the last thousand years thanks to an evil witch. The next, they'd found themselves whisked away through a portal to this cold room in what appeared to be a castle. Even though their banishment was now at an end, Sulphur couldn't help herself. Her murderous instincts took over when she stepped out of the portal and saw the man in the scarlet cloak. The attack was swift, brutal, and thorough. Now, the choked man stared out blankly at the ceiling. Whatever he seemed to be looking at, it wasn't anything on this plane of existence.

"Let's gobble him up," Gravel said, her scratchy voice echoing off the brick walls of the chamber. She began to dance, her arms making circles in the air above her upturned snout, her feet pounding out a rhythmic tattoo on the floor. "Feast on his shank. Strip his skin and sizzle it like bacon. Fricassee his heart with turnips and vinegar."

That's your answer for everything, Sulphur wanted to say, gawking at her sister's plump hips. Their banishment had done nothing to diminish Gravel's waistline—she could certainly stand to lose a pound or two. Sulphur paid no mind to the rumbling in her own belly. Right now, there were more important things to worry about. She tiptoed to the edge of the pentagram that encircled the chamber floor. Drawing in a deep breath, she eased a clawed toe out over the crudely painted line, and then beyond. There was no painful zap, no mystical bolt of energy striking her from the blue. She stepped out of the circle and exhaled. At last, they were free.

"Let's lick him and kiss him," said Dungwort, who had crawled up onto the fallen man's body. Her forked tongue slithered down his earlobe. "Love him and grope him and do many dirty things to him." Her fingers tangled in the curls of his long, white beard. She worked her hands down his torso and between his legs. The folds of the man's cloak flipped open as she reached inside. "Oy, sisters. We do love a stiff one, don't we?"

"Enough!" Sulphur clapped her hands. The sharp retort echoed off the castle walls. Her sisters turned their eyes in her direction, their mouths agape. "Leave him be."

"Why?" her sisters cried.

"We are hungry!" Gravel wailed.

"We are horny!" Dungwort moaned.

Sulphur made her way to the rear of the chamber. The air was rich with the tang of herbs and flowers wafting out from several glass jars. Her hands fluttered over brightly colored beakers and vials on the shelves. This was what humans called a laboratory. It was a place of science and magic. "Clearly our dead friend was a man of great power. Think about it, sisters. He ended our banishment. He pulled us to this place. This was no mere wizard. Perhaps his body will be worth something."

She stopped in front of a wall that served as a library. The shelves were lined with hundreds of books. She pulled one down and opened it. A tiny cloud of dust puffed up from the yellowed pages.

"What does it say?" Gravel said, drawing closer to Sulphur.

"Tell us, tell us," Dungwort said, following suit.

Sulphur's eyes grew wide. "Spells," she gasped. "More than I've ever seen."

With every turned page, more spells revealed themselves. There were spells for persuasion. Spells for beauty. Spells for power.

"Here," Sulphur said, smoothing out the page. "This is what we need." Her pointed ears twitched with excitement. "A duplication spell."

Her sisters stared at her blankly.

Sulphur sighed. "Need I remind you, we are unable to reproduce, as we are all females? Need I also remind you of a certain incident that eradicated all goblin males?" She turned her piercing red eyes to her portly sister.

Gravel stared nervously at the ground. The green skin of her cheeks darkened as she blushed. "I said I was sorry."

"Nevertheless," Sulphur said. "With these spells, I can double our number. Nay, I can triple them, and more."

The dumb expressions on her sisters' faces told Sulphur they had no idea what she was talking about. Indeed, a spindle of drool dripped from the corner of Dungwort's mouth.

"What I'm telling you is that our dead friend has provided us the tools to make ourselves legion. Think of it: an entire goblin army! Thousands upon thousands of us razing this world to the ground. Under our fearsome might, all we desire will be ours."

"Food!" Gravel said.

"Men!" Dungwort added.

"Everything!" Sulphur shouted.

"Then it's lucky for mankind that I'm here to stop you," a voice said from across the room.

The goblins jumped all at once.

It was their corpse, the man in the scarlet cloak. He was floating in the air several feet above the ground. He was hale and hearty, like he'd never been attacked at all. The gouges on his neck were healed. His eyes were no longer bulging with the onset of his painful death. Now they shone with a bright intensity, his irises bursting with sparking light.

"But how..." Sulphur said.

"I'd hardly be known as Merlin the Great if I was unable to cast a simple illusion spell, now would I?"

The magician made a series of quick, nimble movements with his hands. Golden energy pulsed from his fingertips and leaped across the room. Before the goblins could defend themselves, the energy transformed into golden ropes, which bound the goblins where they stood. The ropes crackled and sizzled against the goblins' skins.

With another wave of the magician's hands, a fire ignited across the room. Until now, this corner had been drenched in shadows. The goblins could clearly see the stacked pile of kindling that fed the fire, and the large iron cauldron that sat above it.

"You see, I've discovered a spell that will bring me immortality," the magician said. "The main ingredient is ictythin, a substance that's found only in one place—the marrow of goblin bones. It's extracted with the application of heat. Excessive heat, to be exact."

"No!" the goblins shrieked. An invisible force was pulling them across the floor. They struggled against their bonds and scratched at the floor, but it was no use.

"Now," the magician said with a wry smile. "Who's in the mood for goblin stew?"

CASTLEMAKER

Like a mason of love, you built me into the castle of your desires. Your trowel spread compliments like mortar. Your hands eased my bricks into place with care and affection. This is how you willed me into being. No longer would I be a nothing boy. Where my old body existed, a new structure stood.

"How grand you've become," you said, "the envy of all the castles in the kingdom." With your trained eye, you inspected every square foot of my property. My ramparts were mighty, unyielding. My moat sparkled like the bluest sea. In my dungeon, you unshackled my love, introducing me to pleasures I lacked the courage to explore. Your presence filled every nook and cranny of my fortress, wrapping me in a cocoon of adoration and comfort.

And the sparkle in your eyes when you strutted me before your peers, a preening thing in need of admiration. "Castlemaker," they said in unison, "you've done it again."

Curse me for a fool, not knowing what that meant.

I should have known the score when you encouraged them to trample across my pristine halls. My tender portcullis burned with their heady stench: musk, cigar smoke and bourbon. Their lecherous jeers echoed throughout my chambers. Their filthy handprints stained my impeccable carpets. Dutifully, I turned a blind eye to their crassness. Deep under my moorings, my heart pined only for you.

Time passed, as only time can do, and cracks appeared in my once-impeccable façade. My walls became dulled, weatherbeaten, decrepit. Was this the moment you lost interest in your creation? The tender caresses I craved from you, once so warm, grew cold and distant. Halfheartedly, you mended the fissures you found unappealing, buttressed up my sagging walls. But your touch told me everything—a lover always knows.

You left me for months to visit nearby lands, leaving me to wallow in sadness. I sobbed until my foundations flooded, thinking no one could hear me. A dove living in my spires took pity. To her kind face, I told my story. She wagged her beak in disbelief, consoled me with her delicate feathers. One day, she approached me.

"In return for the shelter you provide, allow me to spy on him."

She flew away. I thought I'd never see her again—the brave little thing. True to her word, she kept her promise.

I almost wish she hadn't.

On a beach off the coast of Spain, she saw you touring an ancient castillo, your eager fingers fluttering over the pitted sandstone walls. In England, you visited a mighty stone keep, your cheeks throbbing pink with desire. In Italy, became enchanted by a noble mott and bailey that smelled richly of limestone and oleander.

When you returned, I confronted you. Caught off guard, you screamed until my tapestries trembled. Your face contorted with rage, you stormed across my drawbridge, saying you were leaving for good.

"To build a new castle," or so the dove said.

I hear he's lovely, an architectural marvel. I hear he's made of the finest stone money can buy. I hear he's lush with fragrant gardens, orchards, and pathways.

You'll survive, you told me before you left. Your heart will find a way.

You were wrong, though.

My moat lays neglected, the waters stagnant and overgrown. Mold creeps across my stone walls. The ghost of our love roams my halls at night, wailing in misery.

But the dove and I have a plan.

She will fly to you once again. She will tell you I'm dying—at least this is true. She will tell you my final request is to see you once more before I pass from this world. In your hubris, you will accept the invitation. You won't be able to resist seeing me brought to ruin.

Once you are inside my walls, I shall perform the final act of our tale. In a shocking display of willpower, I will bring down what's left of me. Brick by brick and wall by wall, I will shake, rumble and roar until I crumble to pieces, burying you under a mountain of shattered stone.

    We'll be together, my love.

    If not in life, then in death.

    The dove will tell our tale, and our story will live forever.

THE AFTERMATH

The day Stacy exploded
was an ordinary day in fall
more or less
the air crisp and cool
the sun dotting the sky
over the schoolhouse
like a blob of orange marmalade
on a child's blue jumper.

In the cafeteria
Stacy sat alone
at her table in the corner
staring at the wall
so the other kids
wouldn't have to see
her big ugly nose
and her tiny breasts
and the hairy birthmark on her cheek
and her Coke-bottle glasses.
Only twelve years old
and already cozy
with the idea of being different,
the notion of self-hatred.

With a sad and lonely sigh
she opened her sack lunch
and instead of the usual meal
—a dry bologna sandwich

made in haste
by her alcoholic mother
who beat her once a week
at the trailer park
where the two of them lived in misery—
instead of *that,*
out popped a roach
the size of a man's thumb.

In the blink of an eye,
the repulsive thing
raced up her arm
and into the sleeve of her blouse
where it disappeared from sight
and skittered around her tummy
in ever-frantic circles,
it's spindly legs clawing
against her bare flesh,
a primordial knot of horror
filling Stacy's tummy.

All at once
she jerked up
and screamed bloody murder,
yanking off her blouse,
her glasses flying,
her arms pinwheeling,
her body spinning in circles
like a dog chasing its tail
as she tried to sweep
the terrified insect
from her underdeveloped body.

And all of the kids laughed and pointed
especially Bobby Meadows
—whom she immediately suspected
had hidden the roach
in the first place—

he was doubled over
snorting, guffawing,
slapping his knees,
tears of joy falling from his eyes.

Well, Stacy was crying too
but with different kinds of tears,
her skin grew hot
and that horror inside
twisted into a
deep and powerful hatred
and burst open
like an abscessed sore
spewing its wet hot infection
into this stupid world.

Stacy went supernova.

(Nobody knew why.
They said later
her father had worked
at a nuclear facility
although Stacy never knew him.
Like, who could keep track of
all the men going in and out
of her Mama's trailer door?)

When she did
it sounded like a giant
stomping the earth under its heel
and the school's walls melted
and ninety-eight mouths were
silenced instantly,
the bodies left behind
like little smoking logs
all that lost potential.

Even downtown

houses shook on their beams
and dust and plaster
rained from ceilings
car sirens blared
streetlamps shattered
the air thick with chalky smoke
while birds dropped to the ground,
thunk, thunk thunk.

When they found her
in that crater
that used to be the school
dazed and drooling,
the clothes singed from her body,
her glasses melted
to a slab of metal
that used to be a table
there was,
it was later said,
the faintest smile on her lips.

Anyway, nobody teased her anymore after that.

HUNGRY

The night Will Graves saw the meteor, there was nothing unusual about him, biologically speaking; nothing remarkable about his emotions—except for the sadness from losing his father the previous year from throat cancer, a terrible way to go. Other than that, he was normal for a teenage boy of medium build and average intelligence. Certainly there was nothing unusual about his appetite.

He was trudging home from his friend Otis's house, hoping he'd be able to put on a smile for his mother's sake, when the ball of light came from behind. It streaked through the cloudless night with a flash so bright he could make out the pinecones on the trail floor, some beer cans, a few cigarette butts. He gasped out loud as the object zoomed off toward the horizon and disappeared behind a line of trees. Will stood there staring, realizing how lucky he was to be there in that exact moment, and it wasn't until he heard the impact that his heart started to race.

Otis's house was only five minutes away. Should he turn back for him? No, his best friend wouldn't believe him. He'd laugh, thinking it was a joke. Otis wouldn't be convinced until Will dragged him out to the woods to show him the crater, the glowing red rock embedded there, smoke rising into the air like satin ribbons.

Or he could make the discovery on his own.

If he did, surely things would surely be different at school tomorrow. He and Otis were pretty much outcasts, but after tonight, he would be "the guy who saw the crater first". People would line up to be his friend. No more hanging out with only Otis, he'd have tons of people to talk to.

When he arrived in the field, there were no splintered trees, no smoking crater, and no signs of an impact anywhere. After an hour of searching, he headed home, his heart sagging with disappointment.

***

There was nothing about the incident on any of the stations, leaving Will to wonder if he was the only person who'd seen it. The meteor had crashed nearby, he was certain. Two nights later he headed out again after his mother had left for work. He hurried toward the trail with his gaze turned upward, hoping for more interstellar action. Which is why he didn't see the stranger at first. He heard him soon enough, though, groaning in the woods near the ditch.

Will figured it was a drifter. A drunk, from the sound of it.

The man emerged under the yellow glow of a streetlamp. He was stumbling about, his arms twitching and jerking like a marionette. *A druggie,* Will thought. *Or a lunatic.* Either way, Will crossed to the other side of the road for good measure. As the distance between them closed, he got a better look at the man. The man's eyes bulged out of their sockets, his tongue was hanging out like a giant gray earthworm, and his emaciated flesh clung to his skeleton.

Will thought maybe he should call 911. He reached for his cellphone and remembered he'd left it at home.

The stranger charged in that moment, bringing with him an awful smell of death and decay. Before Will could scream, the man grabbed him. Powerful hands clamped down on his head, pulling him. The drifter's wild eyes fixed upon his, and his lips bared back to reveal bleeding gums and gnashing teeth. Will managed to jerk his face away as the man chomped down at the base of his skull. Will felt skin tearing, felt the warm surge of blood on his neck and shoulders, and he kicked and struggled but the man held him fast. Before his consciousness slipped away, Will saw a pair of headlights coming around the bend and a car door flinging open, a policeman stepping out. There was a gunshot. Bam! Then two more, Bam! Bam!

The stranger's head exploded in a spray of bone and blood.

Will surrendered to darkness.

***

"My miracle boy," sobbed his mother on the day he finally woke up in the hospital. He listened drowsily as she sat at his bedside, explaining to him what the doctors had told her. He'd lost a lot of blood after the attack, and the ER doctors had worked on him for over an hour. "Finally, your heart started beating again," she said, her hands shaking and tears streaking down her cheek. "They don't know how you did it."

Intravenous fluids kept him sated while he recovered.

Finally, he was ready for solid food. His nurses brought him dinner—a few slices of turkey, a mound of mashed potatoes—before returning to their stations. He ate his meal in peace. But the food tasted bland and unsatisfying. Worse, it settled inside him like bits of jagged glass, and he staggered to the toilet to vomit.

Eager to get home, he never mentioned the incident to anyone.

The next morning, the doctors released him.

He couldn't bear to see his mother cry anymore, so he didn't bring it up when the same thing happened that night after dinner.

And breakfast the following day.

And lunch.

When his stomach finally settled again, Will realized—finally—he was working up an appetite.

***

Will was starving.

Also it hurt to move. And he had a throbbing headache.

He lay in bed tossing and turning when the idea first hit him.

Clenching his teeth against the pain, he eased open the window and snuck out. He moved quietly in the darkness, slipping through brambles and wet grass until he reached the road. The carcass of a dead squirrel lay at his feet, its hind quarters flattened by a passing car. Will stooped over, his hands moving as if possessed by an external force. Within seconds, he'd cracked the rodent's head open and was nibbling on the walnut-sized nugget of meat inside.

The next morning he woke in his bed to find the squirrel's blood caked under his nails.

In the bathroom on his knees, he hoped the running bathwater would cover the sound of his sobbing.

***

Will made every attempt to hold off on his feedings for as long as he could, but the longer he waited the worse the pain got. His head pounded, and his joints grew stiff, threatening to lock up. He didn't look so hot, either—his eyes protruded from their sockets, and his skin grew sallow and smelled sour, like decay. *Just like the guy who attacked me*, Will thought. By the end of the third day, Will was unable to bear his hunger any longer. Sneaking out at night, he roamed the neighborhood until he found a rotting possum in a neighboring alley. Not far from that, he found a dead dog near the highway. Will sighed as he ate, each fetid morsel of rotting brains relieving him more and more of his agony.

The next morning, he scrubbed at his tongue with a toothbrush. When he finally dared to glance in the mirror, his complexion looked normal again.

***

Eventually, the brains of dead animals no longer satisfied him. His nighttime excursions led him to local graveyards, where he searched for fresh graves. Like a dog on all fours, he dug through yards of dirt with his bare hands, using strength he'd never possessed before, scratching and scooping until he reached the coffins below. Then smashing through thin walls of pine and mahogany, he dragged corpses out of their eternal resting places, bashing their heads open to feast on the brains inside. He winced as he ate; decomposing brains were tough and had an irony taste to them, like licking an old battery. But they made the buzzing stop and eased the pain in his aching limbs.

Later in his room, Will held a photograph of his father, traced the outline of his likeness with his finger. The photo had been taken years ago, before the cancer had set it. In the glass, Will could see his reflection superimposed. How much the two looked alike: the flat blond hair, the solid jaw, the eyes set a little too close together. "Something's happening, dad," he whispered. "Something awful."

During the daytime, Will ate in front of his mother, regurgitated it later in secret. At night, he stole out to sate his real hunger.

***

Will became well enough to go back to school, but he didn't want to go.

By now, the story of the attack had made it around town. He was thankful for Otis, who seemed to sense his unease, and promised to walk with him on his first day back. Stepping inside the school, a lump formed in Will's throat. The students who had gathered in the foyer stopped to stare at him. Will's mouth went dry, and he became mindful of the new scar at the base of his neck—the skin graft, still healing.

He turned back to the door. Maybe he should call his mom, convince her that he wasn't quite recovered...

When the first student started clapping, Will didn't understand what was going on, but then another student joined in, then another. Soon the foyer filled with their applause. Will's cheeks flushed when he realized it was for him. Otis smiled, slowly guiding Will through the crowd.

"Graves, my man!" someone shouted.

Someone whistled, another patted him on the back.

But the best moment of all was when Becca Carlson approached him. He had admired her for years, but never had the nerve to approach her. She hugged him, and her chestnut-colored hair spilled onto his face "Everyone's glad you made it," she said.

For Will, it ended up being the best school year ever.

***

May came. It was time for school to end and summer to begin.

With finals approaching, with all the time he'd been spending with Becca, Will hadn't fed in four days. It was the longest he'd ever gone, and now he was ravenous. His head pounded; it felt like bees buzzing there, a terrible droning inside his skull. He sat in his bedroom pretending to study until his mother left for work. Through the open window, he could feel a late evening breeze pushing away the remaining heat of the day.

Soon he heard his mother's car purring in the garage. He got up too quickly, his frozen knee joints popping like firecrackers. Making his way to the window, he watched her car's taillights disappear into the darkness. Back in his bedroom, he slipped into a black sweat suit and jerked a dark knit hat onto his head, and then made his way into the living room, his stomach gurgling and twitching all the way.

"Settle down," he said. "Dinner's coming."

He turned off the outside lights and opened the front door.

Otis was standing there clutching a textbook and a ratty three-ring binder.

Both boys jumped. The binder flopped open, spilling loose paper onto the doormat.

Will snatched the hat off his head and thrust it deep into his pocket. "What are you doing here?"

Otis gathered up the papers and stood again to look at Will. "Thought we could study for the history exam. I know, should have called first. But your grades have been lousy lately. You know, since the..."

"You can say it, Otis. Since 'the attack.'"

"Will, if you fail tomorrow, you'll have to repeat 10th grade. What's Becca going to think then?"

Will opened his mouth to protest, but the buzzing got louder. It was becoming difficult to think.

Otis squinted. "Why are you dressed like a ninja?"

"I'm, ah, going jogging."

"Right now? Do it tomorrow. Tonight, we exercise your brain." He pushed his way into the house. "You coming?"

An owl hooted from the woods nearby. Will wanted to scream at Otis. He wanted to say a million different things other than what he said next.

"Yeah," he offered meekly. He followed Otis inside and closed the door behind him.

**

In the kitchen, Otis was rummaging through the pantry. He seemed to always know where Mrs. Graves kept the good stuff. Grunting with pleasure, he emerged with a bag of potato chips, tore it open. "You hungry?" he asked.

The words hung in the air.

Had it been a harmless question, or...

Will crossed the kitchen and stared at his own reflection in the window. The buzzing ramped up while Otis munched another handful of chips. The noise sounded like a giant stomping through a gravel pit. Will grabbed at the counter to steady himself.

"You okay?" Otis asked.

Will lied. "Sure."

Otis shrugged and took a seat at the kitchen table.

"How about we get started?" he said, motioning for Will to sit next to him. "First question: Which tribe of warriors, fueled by starvation and natural disasters within their own walls, invaded and conquered most of Asia and Eastern Europe in the 13th century?"

A pang of hunger erupted inside of Will, starting in his gut and radiating out to his nerve endings. His skin felt like it was on fire.

Otis, staring.

"I don't know," Will said.

"The Mongols, bro. That was an easy one." Otis looked around the room and crinkled his nose. "Dude, it reeks in here. Mind if I let some air in?"

Will shrugged.

Otis slid open a window, letting the muggy night air settle into the room. He sat down, took out a pen and started doodling on a piece of paper. Then he took a long look at Will and pushed the binder aside.

"We need to talk," Otis said.

"About?"

"You haven't been yourself lately. Not since that night."

"People come back to life, man. It happens."

"Right," Otis said. "On TV shows, or in comic books." He looked down to find the ink had leaked on his fingers. Casually, he rubbed his fingers on his jeans.

"I don't know what to tell you," Will said. "Just got lucky, I guess."

"There's like a 0.5% chance of that actually happening in real life," Otis said.

Will stared back. Otis's cheeks had gone red.

"I'm sorry," Otis said. "I got carried away. Anyway, tell me what happened to the guy who attacked you."

"Not much to tell," Will said. "They weren't able to identify him. Just some bum, I guess. They don't know why he singled me out. Because I was there, probably."

Silence. Otis, glaring.

"Look, that's not all," Otis finally said. "I don't suppose you've heard about 'the brain snatcher'? It's been all over the news. Someone, or some*thing*, has been digging up coffins all over town. Desecrating corpses. Stealing *brains*. Strange, huh? That it all started after you got out of the hospital?"

"Otis, this is—"

"Let me finish," Otis said, thumbing the pen into his shirt pocket. "You've been acting weird lately. I can't remember the last time I've seen you eat something. And I've been watching you, Will. Over the course of a few days, you seem to go through a cycle. You start to get all thin and sickly-looking, and moody. And you smell bad sometimes, buddy. Sometimes you smell like death warmed over." He lifted his shirt to his nose. "You smell bad right now."

Will didn't smell anything. "Your point?"

"So, over the course of a few days your body gets all, *weird*. And wouldn't you know? These spells of yours coincide with the string of graveyard incidents. Every time this vandal strikes—well, the next day, the smell is gone and you're okay. Everything's back to normal. For a while. Until it starts all over."

Will felt like the walls were closing in. He gripped the edge of the table for balance and stood up.

Air. He needed some.

Otis stood up, too. A breeze filled the curtains and they billowed behind him like a shroud. "Dude," he said, "we don't know anything about the guy who attacked you. What if there was something wrong with him?" His voice trembled and he looked as if he were about to cry. "Will, what if he was a *zombie*?"

"Seriously?" Will huffed.

"Maybe you actually died that night. Maybe you came back to life as one of the undead, cursed to eat brains in order to survive."

"Jesus," Will interjected. "There's no such thing as—"

Otis would not be silenced. "I've been reading about it. Zombies have to eat brains to keep their own bodies from decomposing. I figured if it happened to you, then maybe you'd want to be a good zombie, you know, instead of an evil one. You'd probably hold off on the hunger as long as possible. But eventually, you'd have to give in. And when you finally did, you'd never want to hurt anyone or anything. You'd probably force yourself to live off of things that were already dead. Brains from corpses, stuff like that."

"Man, there's no such thing as zombies, okay? If that guy were a zombie, where would he have come from?"

"I don't know. Terrorists, maybe. I don't have all the answers. But I can't find any other way to explain it." Otis's face screwed up and he looked like he was about to cry. "Something's happened to you," he said, his voice cracking. "You're different now, is all."

An ink spot had formed on Otis's shirt pocket. Will said nothing, only watched the stain expanding across the whiteness, slowly spreading outward.

"I want you to do something for me," Otis said, sniffling. "I want you to stand right there and tell me I'm wrong. Look me in the eyes and tell me you're not a zombie."

Will felt the world tilt under his feet. Sweat broke out on his forehead, liquid fire on his already hurting skin. His heart was beating in his head, causing the bees to buzz louder. He wanted to break something, wanted to run out into the night to feed.

Also, some part of him wanted to surrender. He was tired of being a freak, tired of foraging for rotting brains in the dark like some kind of monster. Maybe he should come clean with Otis. Maybe then, the nightmare would end. On the other hand, who knew what the world would do to him? He might wind up in some hospital. Or a lab. He didn't want to be some scientist's guinea pig. What would they do, with their scalpels and saws, to find out the science behind his condition?

"Dude," Will said flatly, "Stop reading so many comic books."

For a moment, Otis seemed like an air mattress with a hole in it. After a moment, he looked up, offered a wan smile. "I guess I sound a little wacky right now," he said. "Sorry I brought it up."

The hunger inside Will settled into a dull ache. For the next few hours, he tried to ignore the dreadful droning of the bees.

***

In the morning, the hunger had intensified into a white-hot flame that tempered Will's every thought. He became vaguely aware of Otis's voice saying it was time to leave for school. Otis grabbed some cookies from the kitchen and the boys set out, taking the trail through the woods. The sun shone like an angry god, sending hot needles of pain into Will's skull.

"Beautiful morning," Otis said, coming to a stop on an embankment overlooking a creek. He put his hands on his hips like some fat mountain adventurer. Sunlight peeped through the line of pine trees and glinted across his hair, crowning him in a halo of dirty gold. "What a view," he said.

Will could no longer hear Otis over the droning. The bees were furious. Someone had kicked up their nest.

Otis tossed a pebble into the creek. "I'm sorry about all that stuff earlier, man. I shouldn't have doubted you."

Will couldn't hear him. Silent as a mouse, he removed his shirt, tossing it to the dirt. The same thing happened with his shoes, his pants. Otis turned in time to see Will, wild eyed and naked, charging toward him.

"What—" Otis said.

Will's hands locked around Otis's neck, choking. Otis toppled backward, falling with a thud on a flattened boulder. Will landed on top of him, a growl forming in his throat. With terrible fury, he smashed Otis's head onto the rock below. There was a sound like ice cracking. Will repeated the action swiftly once more and Otis's leg twitched and then stopped moving.

Will's fingertips sank into the broken skull, digging and prying, the bone snapping away like eggshell. His probing fingers found their mark, sinking deep into the fresh cranial matter. The gore glistened in the sunlight as his trembling hands lifted it to his hungry lips.

The taste was *intoxicating*.

The meat was warm, almost pulsing. And the texture was unlike anything he'd ever tasted. Fresh brains weren't tough like dead animal brains. They were spongy, melting against his quivering tongue. Already, he could feel the pain in his head and limbs subsiding.

When he had scraped out the last bits of his meal and licked his fingers clean, he dragged Otis's body into the bushes and made his way down to the creek. Covered in blood, he washed himself off and quickly got dressed.

***

Will made it to class just as the bell was ringing. He took his seat in the back row next to Otis's empty chair. Mr. Holladay handed out the exams. "Does anyone know where Mr. Collins is today?" he asked. Will glanced at the door and shrugged.

Mr. Holladay signaled for the final to begin. From two rows over, Becca winked at Will, curling her hair playfully around her finger. Soon, every student in the room was working on the test. Except for Will, who stared casually around the room. Mr. Holladay looked at him quizzingly. Then, with a furrowed brow, he turned his attention to a stack of papers on his desk.

At that moment, Will couldn't have cared less about world history. School didn't matter, not anymore.

He was staring at all of the beautiful heads around him, carefully studying the perfect, bony craniums atop those young, unknowing shoulders. His mouth watered as his eyes caressed every delicate indention, every line, every curve, thinking that only a bit of hair, skin, and a thin wall of bone separated him from the warm, savory meals inside.

A thread of drool dribbled onto his lap.

He would never go hungry again.

LOVING THE BEAST

Before you judge me, just know I had reasons for what I did. When you're born looking the way I do, life doesn't hand you many romantic opportunities.

You think I don't know how I look? Please. I see the scar every morning when I look in the mirror. That harelip I was born with never would go away, even though the doctors tried. Two operations in my childhood, and I've still got a tangle of gnarled skin between my lip and my right nostril. Not the most kissable sight you ever did see. Now, I'm not saying I blame my lonely situation on the scar, mind you. Even without it, I've never been mistaken for a looker. God didn't do me any favors when I was born. Broad shoulders. Thick waistline. Hair that's too dull and scraggly to ever be considered pretty. Oh, the kids at school put me through it growing up, don't you just know it. When it comes to insults, I purty near heard 'em all.

Hag. Dogface. Fugly.

Hey, wipe that look off your face. Tessa McRee don't need your pity. I was doing just fine on my own, thank you very much.

Or at least, I thought I was.

This all happened in my tiny house on the outskirts of Texarkana, which, you know, is practically in the middle of nowhere. It's a good place to live if you love the outdoors, in the daytime at least. Miles of quiet in every direction, nobody around but simple folk tending their pastures, everything smelling fresh and clean like pine trees and cow manure.

Nights now, that's a whole 'nother story. It can get a bit spooky for a gal living on her own, so far from the downtown lights and the sky so big and black you feel like you're the last person at the edge of the world. There's all kinds of critters in 'em woods. All of 'em wild and howling and carrying on doing God knows what.

The upside was my parents left me the house when they died and enough money to get by. I rarely went into town, except for groceries. I got lonely sometimes, sure, but I didn't have no man telling me what to do. Hell, I didn't even have to shower every day if I didn't feel like it. But I always do, I got my sense of decorum, you know. I like to shower at night so I can crawl under the covers all soft and clean. Which is where this story begins. In the shower, I mean. There I was, all lathered up and washing my possibles when I heard somebody breathing outside my window.

Hnrrr, hnrrr, hnrrr...

Let me tell you, my flesh went all goosey from the small of my back to my shoulder blades. My shower's got this window what looks out into the backyard. It was a pleasant night, so the window was cracked open and my blinds were up—. Don't you look at me like that. They're always up. Hell's bells, why *wouldn't* they be? My backyard nudges right up to the woods and ain't nothing out yonder but woods as far as the eye can see.

Now, when I heard that sound, I figured somebody'd come out here to get their jollies. A Peeping Tom or whatever them perverts are called. Though why anyone would ever want a look at my ugly mug is beyond me. Somehow I got the nerve up to squint out the window. Sakes alive, I almost pissed myself when I saw a pair of eyes looking back at me.

I had a peeper, all right. But I was pretty sure his name wasn't Tom, or anything else human.

These were beastly, savage, animal eyes.

I hollered and yanked the shower curtain around me, damn near lost my footing in all the fuss. When I looked back out, the face was still there. Darndest thing I ever did see.

It was Bigfoot. Sasquatch. Whatever you call it.

Yeah, I'd always thought he was a myth too. I'd heard stories of campers and hunters seeing him around these parts but never believed 'em. You got them TV shows like *Mountain Monsters* which is basically a bunch of hillbillies stomping through the woods toting rifles and acting like they're drunk on moonshine. Then they never finding anything. I mean, gimme a cotton-picking break.

Now, finding the real monster in your own backyard? Christ on a saltine cracker, it scared the bejeezus out of me. My heart was pounding so hard I almost couldn't think straight. This dark hairy mass of fur towered over me, as big as an ape and twice as ugly, its copper-colored eyes shining in the darkness like a pair of headlights

They say if you see a wild predator in the woods, like a bobcat or bear, you make yourself as big as you can. You hoot and holler real loud in the hopes of scaring 'em away. But I was frozen with fear. One wrong move could trigger him. If he'd wanted to kill me, he sure as hell could've. Wasn't nothing but a pane of glass between us, no match for a brute his size.

He didn't, though.

As my eyes adjusted, I realized why he was breathing so hard.

This motherfucker was masturbating!

My hand to God, he was playing with himself down there, working his hand back and forth over his pecker like a horny teenager with a porno mag.

Looking back now, I shoulda grabbed my gun. I shoulda called 911 or run. I shoulda done any number of things instead of what I did.

So, what'd I do?

Well, I wrapped a towel on and slipped out to get a better look. Ain't never seen anything like it before, and I was curious.

He was still by my window. He had a massive chest with a somewhat rounded back, long arms that hung almost to his knees and thighs like tree trunks. At least he'd stopped jerking it, thank God. We stood there staring at one another. Him at me. Me at him.

As his eyes bored at me from under that broad, sloping forehead, my unease started to melt like a pad of butter on a stack of hotcakes. I can't explain it. There was nothing threatening in his gaze. The opposite, actually. He ducked his head down level with his massive shoulders, a kind of sheepish look in those big round eyes. I got the feeling he was ashamed to have been caught doing what he was doing. When I realized that, I looked at him like you would look at a stray dog, something like pity filling my heart. Which I suppose, he could sense, maybe? Animals pick up on things you and I can't, they say. He wrung his big ape hands together and his nostrils kind of twitched, and that's when I figured out the expression on his face.

He was *fascinated* with me.

I got a little self-conscious, if you want to know the truth. My body, flawed though it is, had never been adored like that. He stepped toward me. I eased back a bit, not out of fear, more because I didn't know what else to do. He kept on coming. There was no place for me to go but the house, so that's where I went. He followed me inside, had to crouch a bit to get under the door frame. I can't describe how it felt to have this huge critter in my house, a private space that was mine alone, my sanctuary from this cruel world and all the horrible people in it. I got a good whiff of him then. He smelled a bit like a dog, you know, animal-like but not unpleasant. There was also a sweet scent about him which I figured was the smell of the forest clinging to his dark brown fur: verbena, honeysuckle and such. I was aware of my heartbeat thudding in my chest and next thing I knew the towel was off and we fell on my bed and he was on top of me and that's how it all started.

Now listen, I'm not the kind of girl who'd ever done this before. I mean, I'd heard talk of the locals here having sex with animals. This is Texarkana we're talking about. The people around here ain't exactly royalty. A ranch hand is likely stick it to one of the barnyard critters he's tending to when nobody else is around, all those poor cows and sheep walking around all bow-legged, Lord Almighty. And don't think for one minute that some of those rich housewives on the other side of town don't spread peanut butter on their hoo-hahs and let Fido go to town when their husbands are away. Hell!

No, this wasn't something I'd ever dreamed I'd do. But there I was, almost forty and hadn't had a man all proper-like my whole entire life. Last time was that blowjob I gave Chucky Wilcott in the janitor's closet in school. And he was drunk on malt liquor and then denied it afterward, so it really kind of don't even count.

It's not like the creature was a pure animal, not all the way through, like other animals are. Sure, he was shaped different from me and draped in fur from his head to his gigantic feet, but there was something strangely human about him. You know how scientists say mankind evolved from monkeys? I kept wondering if this fella was maybe the missing link or something.

Yeah, we did it, though. It was pretty good, too. Excellent, even. Biggy is what I came to call him, for obvious reasons. He came over every night all through the summer, always after the sun went down.

I'd crack the door and wait for him draped across my bed like some lovelorn harlot, wearing nothing but my skimpiest drawers, my skin all softened with lotion and scented candles burning everywhere. I'm not ashamed to say I indulged myself in a lifetime of carnal desires in those months. There was no denying our passion, the urgency of his thrusts, his thick prick splitting me up the middle, filling me up completely, giving me something I'd been lacking all my life, and me, bucking against his strokes, riding him like a hobby horse, my fingers twined in the dense hair on his shoulders, doing my best to hold on. Then after, laying in his strong arms, my face buried in the coarse fur on his chest, his snores echoing in my tiny bedroom, his great nostrils quivering, his jizz drying on my pubes like Elmer's glue.

The next morning, there was always that same sense of dread as the soft morning light crept into the room. Him slowly awakening, his eyes growing at first lucid and then restless with every passing second, me asking him not to leave, him always insisting, me pleading, begging, him pushing me away as he bounded out the door and into the brush.

There was love, at least on my part. During the day, I'd glide through my house giddy as a schoolgirl, humming along to dumb country songs on the radio, spending hours in the kitchen making meals he loved: roasted chickens and pot roast all smothered in gravy, all while enjoying the dull ache between my legs, the lingering ghost of his sex. Then at night, the woozy feeling in my tummy when he showed up in the doorway, the inferno of our surging lust followed by my crude attempts to tame him, teaching him to sit at a table, to eat off a plate, to drink beer out of a can, to spoon me on the couch, nestled against his hulking body, him protecting me while we watched reruns of Maury Povich on the TV, which he loved for some reason, dumb animal that he was.

Yet every morning, he'd leave, and I'd be alone, all over again.

Over time, I realized I was nothing more than a hole for him, a toy to pick up whenever he wanted to play, and possibly one of many, to boot. Sometimes in his fur, I'd smell the lingering hint of rose, a touch of patchouli, a wispy tickle of sandalwood. Was he seeing another woman? Or women?

The heat of our lovemaking began to dim, him getting greedy, more forceful every time, rushing to the finish line and not returning the favor, all slam bam and no thank you ma'am. Then retiring to the couch where he'd sprawl out like a sloth, his testicles hanging like two heavy avocados, guzzling beer after beer and burping and farting like he owned the place. The noises he made when he ate, once sweet and endearing, now turned my stomach, him slurping at his greasy paws, his great jaws cracking chicken bones whole, the gulps of food sliding down his big gullet, until I couldn't take it no more.

One night there at the end of summer, I locked the door and huddled under a table in the dark. He showed up at his usual time and howled and shrieked and thudded at the door with his hammer fists, eventually cracking it, splintered wood flying everywhere, then stumbling inside, mad with desire, pawing at my clothes, his rough hands under my nightshirt, squeezing my tits too hard, and me telling him, No, Biggy, no, and him baring his teeth and panting in my face, going hnhr, hnhr, hnhr, his hot breath like spoiled meat, his prick already angry and swelling, and me slapping his cheeks, me screaming, punching, crying, but those big hairy arms holding me down, and me left with nothing else to do but hoist up my knee as hard as I could, planting 'em in those big nuts of his, him wailing and letting me go, doubling over in pain, and me scrambling for my keys.

The anger I felt inside, the rage of it all had me shaking so hard by the time I got to my Honda I liked to never have got the key in the ignition. A glance over my shoulder fixed that right away, though, the sight of him standing in the doorway, the white glow of the porch light giving him a silvery sheen, beating his huge fists against his chest, howling into the night, spittle flying from his open mouth, his fury echoing over the treetops, startled jackdaws fluttering for safety, and me firing up the engine, wanting to smash my foot on the pedal, to drop it into reverse and slam into him with the car, but instead screaming, screaming, screaming until my throat was raw, and then peeling out the driveway, tears pouring down my cheeks and him in the rearview mirror getting smaller and smaller, and my heart pounding like a jackhammer with anger, sadness, and fear that he might follow, or that he might be there when I returned.

And I drove straight here.

What do you say, Sheriff? I can lead you to him. Want to round up your men? Tell 'em they're going on a different kind of hunt. The kind of hunt those hillbillies on *Mountain Monsters* can only dream of.

THOSE WHO WERE ASLEEP

One afternoon in his cramped apartment, ninety-six-year-old Marcus Vander curled up on his lumpy bed, let out a long mournful sigh, and died.

He found himself transported to another place. Blinking several times, he took in the beautiful scenery all around. He stood on a verdant hillock. In the distance, a lake sparkled brilliantly beneath majestic, snow-capped mountains. A white, flowing robe covered his body. He glanced at his hands. No liver spots, no wrinkles. The skin was now ruddy and pulled smooth by youthful muscle. Gulping in a mouthful of crisp, healing air, he felt at peace in both mind and body. He curled his toes into warm grass and laughed deeply from strong lungs.

Heaven. The reward of peace for a long, good life. Surely it would be smooth sailing from here.

It was, for a beautiful moment. Until he started thinking: what was the point of all this beauty, if he had nobody to share it with?

Not far away, a dog barked. A white Shih Tzu bounded through the grass toward him, its fluffy tail bobbing along behind.

He knelt. The dog leaped into his arms like she'd done so many times before. "Tiny?" he asked, nuzzling the dog's wet nose. "Is it really you?"

It was. He'd know his favorite pet anywhere. He'd adopted her in the golden time of his life, and she'd lived for fourteen wonderful years. He'd bonded deeply to Tiny, often preferring her company to other people. Others would let you down, but a dog's love was unwavering. Oh, the hole her death had left in his heart. Holding her now, Marcus realized that losing her had led to his own decline. Without Tiny around, he'd stopped caring for himself properly:

missing meals, forgetting his meds. Alone without his pet, life on Earth began to feel like one lonely, never-ending day.

But she was here now.

"The scriptures promised we'd be reunited with our loved ones," a familiar voice said. He glanced over his shoulder to find a woman approaching. She wore a similar robe and appeared to be near his same age. When she smiled, he recognized her instantly.

"Mom!"

"What a glorious day," she said. "Give me a hug."

They embraced. Marcus held her tightly against his chest, a surge of joy erasing the years they'd been apart. Everything felt right again. "I've missed you," he said, choking back tears. "So, so much."

She leaned back to look at his face. "Such a handsome young man."

"Good genes," he said, smiling.

Her eyebrows furrowed. "A bit thin, though. Were you eating enough?"

Marcus felt his cheeks flush with embarrassment. Same old Mom, after all this time. "Sure, I ate just fine."

"A family reunion without me?" a man's voice said.

Marcus froze. The voice sounded younger than he remembered, but there was no question who it belonged to. From across the grassy plain, his father approached, a white robe flowing over his stocky frame.

"David!" Mom rushed forward to greet him. The elder Vander was also restored to a younger state. He appeared to be in his thirties. His full head of hair was neatly combed across his scalp with a neat fade on the sides that gave him an assertive look. He picked up Mrs. Vander about the waist, gave her a playful spin, and then turned to greet his son.

Marcus felt his heart begin to race. Memories of life with his father were returning, and not all of them were pleasant. Mr. Vander practiced corporal punishment in Marcus's upbringing, meaning Marcus received spankings well into his teens, often with a belt. Once, he'd been punched in the face at dinner for chewing too loudly. When his father had finally died of old age in a nursing home, Marcus didn't feel sad. He felt relieved.

"Dad," he said. "You look ... well." Sober, was what he wanted to say.

"Surprised to see me, eh?" David jabbed his finger at the ground with a sideways grin that made Marcus uncomfortable. "Thought I'd end up in that other place?"

Marcus struggled to answer. It was true. In all his contemplations of the afterlife, he never suspected he'd be reunited with someone he feared.

"Me too," his father continued. "Was pretty sure I'd earned a seat at old Nick Scratch's table."

"David," Mrs. Vander scolded. "This is heaven. A fresh start for everyone. Marcus, hug your father."

Marcus dutifully took a step forward, his arms out and open, then he paused. Something twisted in his heart, and he sighed, letting his arms fall to his sides. Mr. Vander stared at him flatly, his feet planted below him, his arms folded against his burly chest. Marcus took a deep breath, then moved forward again. The men managed to pull off a brief, clumsy embrace. It felt more like a reluctant handshake than a show of affection, and Marcus was thankful when it was over.

At their feet, Tiny sensed something amiss, perhaps reading her master's body language. She began to bark. With her teeth bared and her fluffy hair on end, she moved in on the elder Vander. The small muscles in her legs flexed and she jumped at him, chomping down on his leg.

"Yow!" Mr. Vander yelped.

"Tiny!" Marcus said. "No!"

Using his other foot, his father kicked the dog. Tiny yelped and went tumbling into the grass. David wheeled around, his face red with fury. "Can't you control your damn dog?"

"David!" Mrs. Vander said. "Don't talk to your son that way."

"Quiet!" Mr. Vander smacked her across the face. She collapsed, clutching her hands over her head like a shield.

Marcus squeezed his hands into fists. Even in heaven, it seemed this leopard could not change his spots. "Bastard!" he yelled and hurled himself forward.

Mr. Vander had always been stronger. A solid uppercut across the jaw sent Marcus flying.

Then his father clambered on top of him. With his weight in his knees, he pinned Marcus to the ground. Marcus's eyes welled with tears at the look of hatred blazing on his father's downturned face. Mr. Vander lifted his right fist up high. It came down like a hammer on Marcus's jaw. The left fist followed, then the right again. A few feet away, Tiny crawled out of the grass and started barking again.

"You left me to die in that nursing home!" Mr. Vander said, punctuating each phrase with a blow. "Your own father!"

"David!" Mrs. Vander cried. "You're hurting him!"

Bam. Marcus felt cartilage crack inside his nose. Bam. His lip split open. Bam. He tasted blood. Bam. A tooth splintered. He struggled to sit up, but his father held him fast. "P-please," Marcus tried to spit out.

"Who's the big man now, boy?" his father said, his mouth twisted into a sneer. "Who's the big man now?"

Through swollen eyelids, Marcus glanced upward, searching the heavens for an explanation. He found none, only an endless blue sky and the glory of an eternal, golden sun.

WHEN THE NIGHTMARE ENDS

Heather wakes in the morning and stretches out into the cool, soft sheets, feeling amazing—until she sees the tarantula on the bed. It's a big one. Furry. Black. She can see her own horrified reflection in its many hungry eyes. Her blood turns to ice, her body grows still. The spider tenses in response, mandibles twitching. Heather acts quickly. In one frantic motion, she flings the sheets up with all her might. The spider hurtles across the room, thunks against the wall, falls stunned to the floor. Heather sprints across the room to get a broom or some Raid or a goddam chainsaw or whatever but her heart almost stops when she opens the door. The creepy-crawly fuckers have infested the hallway. They're on the floor, the ceiling, the walls...

She slams the door shut and bolts back into the bedroom. With shaking hands, she manages to claw the window open. A few seconds later, she's out on the ledge, ready to jump.

"Sir," a young man's voice says, echoing across the cavernous chamber. Overhead, a bat stirs, adjusts its grip on the rocky ceiling, and goes to sleep again. "She's getting away."

Johnson is writing the daily quotas on a whiteboard when the comment interrupts him. He sighs and glances at his wristwatch. It's not even an hour into the shift. At this rate, he'll never get to those expense reports today. He tosses the marker onto his desk and scans the room where the employees sit in their headsets and crisp, white shirts, all focused on their monitors—except for the new guy. Voss. He's staring at Johnson with a dumb look on his face. Of course, it would be Voss. Johnson's trudges through the rows of desks, his indigestion flaring.

Voss's monitor is in split-screen mode. One side shows the target's driver's license photo. The other shows a rendering of her dream, with a few menu options below.

Johnson fishes an antacid from his pocket and pops it into his mouth. "What program are you running?"

"Arachnophobia 2.0."

"Intensity?"

"Forty percent, sir."

"Vitals?"

Voss types a command on his keyboard. The info blips across the screen:

> Subject: Heather Sawyer
> Age: Twenty-four
> Location: Schenectady, NY
> Heart rate: 135 bpm

"Dial up the first program by fifteen percent," Johnson says, crunching the chalky tablet between his back teeth. "Introduce Basophobia at level three."

"L-level three?" Voss asks, wide-eyed. His young face goes white.

"Do it."

"Yes, sir."

Heather looks down from the second-floor ledge. The landing's going to hurt. It's either that, though, or the spiders. She jumps, bracing for the impact. Instead, her feet punch through the lawn like its paper. The darkness below swallows her. She falls and falls and falls, into the all-consuming void. Her heart hammers inside her chest. Focus, *she thinks.* Breathe. *She gulps air into her lungs, and exhales, forcefully, methodically, until she is calm again.*

A rope falls through the air nearby, maybe twenty feet away. She doesn't question where it comes from, only flattens her body like a skydiver and glides toward it. Her hair whips across her face as the rope gets closer. She feels a surge of relief when she catches it, then wishes she hadn't. It's not a rope at all—it's a web strand. Her hands stick to its gluey surface. The more she struggles, the more it clings. Now her arms are tangled in it, her legs, her entire body. And worse, she's being hoisted up like a fish on a hook. She looks up the length of web and into the many eyes of an enormous spider-god.

At last, Heather screams.

Voss's screen flashes. Electricity hums out of the back of the computer through a cable. The cable joins to a bundle of other cables that feed into a hole in the cavern floor.

A smile widens across Voss's face. Johnson pats him on the back. "Nice work."

With the distraction out of the way, Johnson makes his way back to his whiteboard. Quotas first, then the expenses.

***

Only when the last worker is gone does Johnson rest for a moment. He sits quietly at his desk, same as every day. From a drawer, he pulls out a picture frame. The glass is cold to the touch. His eyes sting as he traces over the image of the woman. He chokes back emotions and puts the photo away.

He scans his card into a reader. The elevator takes him down. The chamber he enters is large and dark and cold. Cables slither through a hole in the rocky ceiling and terminate in a large capacitor. Suspended in the air below that, is a jagged fissure made of energy. Electricity crackles and sputters along its edges. The fissure seeps a substance that reminds him of TV static. It hurts to look at. Indigestion twists in his belly like a dying child. His body shivers. This is the part he hates.

He takes a deep breath and pulls a lever on the wall. The gathered energy surges into the capacitor. The fissure hisses and sputters and dilates. Not much, a few inches? Enough for today, anyway.

Johnson steps toward the fissure. Beads of sweat dampen his forehead. An enormous, unblinking red eye glares out from the other side. Gray tentacles wiggle from the hole like worms. Where they probe Johnson's face an ochre slime remains. He swallows hard, and his bowels threaten to loosen.

"A l-little closer today, Master."

A screeching voice that sounds like pain says: "Yesss."

Johnson wipes at his sweating brow. Though he asks it every day, he must do so again. It's a compulsion. "Master," Johnson says, his voice quivering. "Y-you will bring her back? When you finally emerge? You'll bring her back, right?"

"Among many other thingsss."

For Johnson, it's all he needs to hear.

LOSING IT

It wasn't like Ollie Duggins never *tried* to lose the weight. He had, lots of times. He'd spent thousands of dollars over the course of his life on everything from diets to pills to hypnosis. Nothing seemed to work. Eventually, he got used to the feel of his extra bulk: How his thighs rasped together when he walked, the way his body jiggled even after he stopped moving. He got used to the way people stared in public, too. All their snide comments, the snickering. Over time, he simply accepted that he'd be fat until the day he died, and that was all there was to it.

Until that day at work.

The chair.

Thankfully, Ollie rarely thought about his weight on the job, an unexpected benefit of working at the hospital. Most days, he simply stayed too busy. Part of the reason he was such an effective data-entry clerk, his boss told him, was because he didn't socialize with other employees. Instead, Ollie clocked in, plopped down on his chair and got to work. That's what he was doing that Thursday afternoon, when, without warning, his seat groaned beneath him and some vital piece of hardware snapped loose. Ollie was dimly aware of an object flying across the room, dinging off a file cabinet. Next thing, he was tumbling to the floor.

He came to his senses, flat on his back and spread-eagled, staring numbly at the ceiling. Over the swell of his belly, the faces of his co-workers came into view. For one terrible instant, he swore he could hear them holding their collective their breaths.

Then, it started. The laugher.

One giggle turned into another, and soon they were all laughing and pointing. A few even came out of their cubicles to join in.

His boss had been a real prince about it, had silenced them, had helped Ollie back to his feet. Maybe the company needed to invest in better chairs, he'd said. Stop getting the ones that looked so cheap.

But Ollie felt them staring when he punched out for the day. The Fat Guy Who Broke His Seat.

That night, he hurled his dinner plates against the wall.

The first call the next morning was to work, to let them know he wouldn't be coming in today. The next one was to a number he kept at the back of a drawer.

Ollie waited in his car in a questionable part of town. The doctor arrived at last, driving a Mercedes with a rattling muffler. Reaching into the pocket of his designer jogging suit, he pulled out a slip of paper. "It's new," he said. "Works on the central nervous system to suppress the appetite."

Ollie paid him in cash.

Later, in the parking lot of the pharmacy, he thumbed a pill out of the bottle, swallowed it down dry.

By the time he got home, the pill had kicked in, spreading a numbing sensation throughout his body. It felt nice, he thought. Like his skin was melting butter. So, with nothing else on his agenda, he sat down to watch some TV.

He never had the urge to eat that afternoon, not once.

Until later in the evening, when a commercial for a taco joint came on. The camera zoomed in for a slow motion caress of the crispy shell, the steaming glob of beef, the bright layers of lettuce, tomatoes, and sour cream.

To the pill's credit, his stomach never grumbled, but that didn't stop him from wanting the taco. To hell with his stomach, it was his brain that craved the experience. That crunch was all he could think about, all those zesty flavors dancing on his tongue.

Damn, he could almost taste it.

Instead of giving in to his obsession, he got up, forced down another pill.

The numbness intensified until he had to admit, he was feeling pretty good. The pill was unlike anything he'd ever taken. He felt lighter than air, like he was floating.

It was a burger commercial that finally did him in.

He saw it during one of the breaks on *Late Show*. The commercial's director deserved a raise, because the burger was a work of art. The patty was thick and hearty, lined with perfect grill marks. The veggies sparkled with dew, like they'd just come from the garden.

The hamburger sent Ollie crashing back to reality.

He wanted that burger bad.

If not that burger, then *something*.

Anything.

He headed to the kitchen to forage for food, a ritual he'd partaken in hundreds of times. The pill rendered his thoughts muzzy and unfocused, yet he managed to cook up a steak in a skillet, to heat up a baked potato, pile it high with butter and sour cream. He slapped the meal onto a paper plate—thank goodness he hadn't tossed those out—and settled down in front of the TV with the meal balanced on his thighs. Tuning in to a midnight mystery, he let the TV's light flicker over him as became lost in the mechanics of eating.

Cut. Chew. Swallow.

Repeat.

Eating became an automatic action, just something he did to feel better. And dammit, he was feeling content. Everything he needed was right here: A warm dinner, a comfy place to sit, a decent show to take his mind off reality.

Cut. Chew. Swallow.

The steak was better than anything he'd had in a long time. It was tender and delicious. Maybe a bit bloody. Normally, he didn't take his meat so rare, but tonight, all that extra juice really hit the spot.

When the mystery ended—the murderer had been the mistress, just like he'd suspected—the fog in his mind let up a bit, just enough for him to glance down.

He stared at the paper plate, what was left of it.

The plate was torn to ribbons, swimming in a pool of red. The steak was gone, every bit of it. The potato too. Even the skin.

He hadn't stopped there.

The utensils were embedded in a crater he'd carved into the top of his thigh, glistening amid layers of fat and meat. Blood pulsed hot through severed veins, dripping down his legs in rivulets, soaking the carpet under his feet.

He stared at that hole for a very long time.

Then, with the TV droning in the background, he licked his lips, picked up his knife and fork, and cut off another slice.

FAMILY TIME

"There's been an accident," Peter's mother said over the phone. "Your pop's banged up pretty good, so I'm going to sit with him here at the hospital. You'll have to stay at Nana's tonight."

Peter gulped. Through the room's only window, a flash of lightning illuminated the downpour outside. He crossed the cramped, musty room and cupped a hand over the mouthpiece. "*Here? At the old folk's home?*"

"It's not ideal, I know," his mother said. "But the administrator says it's okay, just for tonight."

"But mom..." He looked over at the couch, where his grandmother sat. She was staring blankly into a corner and gesturing with her hands as if she were summoning up an ancient demon. "Nana smells funny."

"Oh, grow up, Peter. You're twelve now, almost a man. It's your Nana, for Christ's sake. Think of it as family time."

Maybe he had loved his Nana at one time, but she had taken a turn for the worse lately. She had gotten so damned old. And there'd been rumors in the family that she'd become obsessed with the occult in her later years. She'd started doing bizarre things. Like talking to people who weren't there and babbling in a strange tongue he'd never heard before. He didn't know much about other languages, but it sounded vaguely like Latin. It freaked him out just to look at her. Her skeletal limbs. The mole on her chin, like a giant, hanging tick. The shock of untamable white hair that made her seem kind of witchy.

What he wanted to say was: *I'm not doing it. Hell to the no.*

But he knew better than to argue. They'd just moved to Arkansas with his father's new job, so there were no other relatives to watch him. Of course, he would have to stay with Nana.

So he did his best to sound brave. "Okay. Tell pop I love him."

Over on the couch, Nana had pulled a prune from one of the pockets of her nightgown. She slurped it at her fingertips like a hungry cannibal feasting on a human heart. Amazing, he'd never noticed how large her mouth was, as if she could swallow her entire hand, python-like. Purple drool dribbled down her fingers and into her lap.

Why had he let his parents convince him it was a good idea to visit Nana while they went out for the evening? Then there was the weird storm that had blown in from out of nowhere. He wished his parents had listened when he urged them it was best for them to call off their date night. Now he'd be stuck there all night.

"You're all mine now, dearie," Nana said, stroking the cushion beside her.

Peter begrudgingly joined her on the couch. She reached out and clamped her hand down over his. The skin felt papery, like it would tear at any moment, but her muscles were surprisingly strong. He looked down. Her hand, with her long, yellowed fingernails and bony fingers, looked like a claw.

They watched a disturbing documentary about serial killers. Nana cackled at inappropriate moments, which made him squirm. Down the hallway, an old man was screaming for his sweet lost kitty.

When it was time to sleep, Peter took over the couch. The snoring started as soon as Nana crawled into her tiny bed: a choking, wet sound like a resurrected corpse gasping for air. Peter listened to the rain's assault on the roof. He stared at the clock for at least two hours, before finally drifting off. He opened his eyes to the sounds of Nana calling out: "Horace! Is that you, Horace?"

Horace was the name of Peter's grandfather.

He'd died long before Peter had been born.

It was going to be a long night.

***

A creaking door woke Peter later, and he heard someone shuffling in the hallway.

He sat up, listening. The only other sound was the rain's relentless barrage on the roof. His eyes adjusted to the dim light of the room.

Nana's bed was empty.

His heart pounded in his chest as he crept to the open door and peeped out into the long, dark hallway.

At the far end, he caught the flash of a leg disappearing around the corner. The leg appeared to be draped in Nana's nightgown.

"Nana?" he called, making his way down the hallway.

Every door he passed was open. The residents inside were missing.

Thunder boomed outside. The hallway lights flickered.

He turned the corner into the recreation room and reeled.

A metallic pile of crutches, wheelchairs and walkers had been shoved into one corner, and a chaotic mess of pajamas, robes, and nightshirts littered the floor.

In the middle of the room, an enormous mound of a flesh undulated and oozed . The residents—all of them were here, fused into one giant throbbing blob. Ancient faces stared out from a tangle of bony arms and legs.

"We've been expecting you," said a croaking, hideous voice. Nana's?

Peter turned to run.

The blob lurched after him, slapping its many limbs against the linoleum floor. Peter was quicker. He reached the front door, pulled it open.

Lightning crashed, revealing two figures. His mother, looking very unhappy. And his father, whole and without injury.

"D-dad?" Peter said.

"Sorry to lie to you, sport," his father said.

"Poor boy," his mother continued. "Every few generations, a sacrifice must be made. It's the flesh of the youth that keeps us forever young."

If he could just make it past them... He flung himself against their bodies, but they were stronger, and held him fast.

Behind him, the organism advanced. "It's family time," the Nana-thing said.

Dozens of claw-like hands scratched into the flesh on his arms, his legs, pulling him as he slid across the floor, scrambling, straining, and fighting, but drawing closer, ever closer to the blob's enormous waiting mouth.

STARSTRUCK

When Devon graduates high school, his momma sighs and cuts him some slack. She thinks it can't have been easy, what with her only son liking other boys, all those years of taunts, the endless bullying. Mostly, she blames herself for raising him without a father. By the end of summer, it's obvious he's suffering from a lack of ambition. Hell, he barely even helps around the house. When she threatens to throw him out, he reluctantly gets a job at the pizza shop, and that's where he meets Billy Quinton.

Yes, that Billy Quinton. Former action star. Notorious heartbreaker. Hollywood bad boy. He's in Idaho (of all places) working on an indie thriller when he staggers in at five to close waving a $100 bill and stinking of vodka. "I'm famished," he tells Devon, with a wink that says *in more ways than one.*

Devon's charmed by the actor's gruff voice and cocky attitude, and they talk until Billy finishes his meal. Then continue to the parking lot. And from there, into the back of Billy's shiny black BMW. The actor knows what to say to get young Devon out of his pants. On the warm leather seats, with moonlight sparkling off a chrome skull pendant hanging from the rear-view mirror, Devon gives himself over to the man who once repelled down the Chrysler Building in his favorite movie, *Skyscraper Rescue.*

In the morning, Devon's momma cries when the actor does donuts in his car in front of her house. But by then her son has already fallen for him. What can she do? Billy smells like cigarettes and he's got a big dick and talks about lunches with Keifer Sutherland. So, off Devon goes, dragging along his ratty suitcase with the busted wheel while his momma wrings her hands on the porch.

And at first, it's wonderful. The parties attended. The cities visited. The pure intoxication of being loved. For young Devon, it's as if he's tamed some kind of wild beast. This eccentric personality with his distinct peculiarities, like the pentagram tattoo on his back, his books on black magic, and the nightly rituals with scented oils and burning candles.

It's not long before Devon sees a different side of Billy. Those bedroom whispers, once so soft and soothing, warp into throaty grunts and urgent demands. Caresses, once so delicate and nurturing, mutate into sadistic slaps and aggressive acts of dominance.

Devon notices other problems, too. Like Billy arguing on the phone with his manager about money problems. One night at Chéz Marie, Billy curses out a waiter when his credit card is denied. And then there's the drinking problem. It's constant. Long nips straight from the bottle. In the daytime, it's gin. Whiskey in the evenings. And when he's drunk, he makes cruel jabs: about Devon's girly hips, his small-town accent and his crooked, crooked teeth. Devon laughs it off at first. What can he do? Then he doesn't say anything. Until one day, in a less-than-stylish motel room outside of LA, he does. For that he gets punched in the face.

Billy screeches off in his car, leaving Devon behind to blink at the carpet. Devon can imagine Billy out there, walking the promenade, his silver Rolex glinting in the moonlight, those hungry boys eyeing the bulge in his jeans. And though this relationship has brought him pain, the thought of someone else having Billy is worse, so he picks up the phone to call him, to say he's sorry, or whatever. He leaves a voicemail. Then another. And another. He's still dialing at midnight when he hears a sound outside.

It's a tinkling sound at first, almost magical. Until he realizes its glass breaking. Devon pulls back the blinds, and heat slams him in the face. Across the courtyard, the other side of the hotel is ablaze. Tongues of flame lick at the walls, warping the windows, causing the glass to buckle, to splinter. He retreats into the hallway, where everyone's panicking and running, saying to get out, get out now. And he starts to. But then he doesn't. He goes back to his room, sits on the bed. It would be a simple thing to just let the fire take him, and for a moment, he considers it. Until a wall of heat comes charging down the hallway, and his mouth fills with smoke. Then he shoves what he can into his suitcase, and escapes by breaking a window.

On the front lawn, he joins the other dazed travelers in their crumpled suits and pajamas and flip flops. Together, they watch the hotel burn. And it isn't until a fire truck is screaming its way toward them that he notices something's moving in the fire. He moves in closer to get a better look while shouting back to the other guests. They look at him like he's crazy. Why won't they listen?

It's a man.

Not just any man. It's Billy Quinton.

Well, it is, and it isn't. It looks like him, but it's some kind of demon. It's got claws instead of fingers and its skin is made of flames, and it's laughing. By then, the firemen are there, and they're pushing back the crowd and spraying at the inferno. But what can they do? The demon is unfazed by the water and he's punching and hitting the walls of the hotel and everything he touches burns brighter.

And is it Devon's imagination, or does he see other figures in the fire? The spirits of other young men, just like him. The demon is kicking and screaming at them, telling them they're pieces of shit, that they're worthless. And they're all lying there, taking it. Every last one of them. Devon crumples to the ground and watches them for hours in the chill of the night with his knees pulled tight against his chest.

By daylight, the air still reeks of smoke but the last of the glowing embers are sputtering. The demon and the other figure are gone. The other guests have left, too, gone one by one, either picked up by taxis, or friends, or having wandered off to other nearby hotels. Devon sits alone on the dewy lawn. He wonders about his life, about how he got here, about where he's headed, about why he's become so used to the feelings of loneliness, of sadness. He's so deep in his thoughts, he's surprised when he feels a hand on his shoulder.

It's Billy Quinton, you bet.

"You look like hell," the actor says, with a squeeze. It's the gentlest of gestures, and somehow it strikes up a deep longing inside Devon's heart again.

Except that hand. It's way too warm. Almost hot.

When Devon looks up into those handsome eyes, he stares for what feels like forever.

Then he gets up and walks away, leaves Billy standing there, listening to the sound of the suitcase's busted wheel as it drags along on the sidewalk.

DEATH BY KITTENS

It ends in a house filled with dozens of litter boxes, all stinking and heavy with waste, maggots thrashing desperately in the putrid stew, flies darting about like kamikaze pilots; and with hundreds of food-caked saucers stacked on the counters, on the floor, on top of other saucers; and with him, gasping for air on his back, his body crushed under a thousand furry bodies, the rough scrape of their tongues on his arms, the weight of them on his throat, their purring in his ears like a drug, lulling him into serenity, as he tells himself: *This is fine.*

A WOMAN'S PLACE

The loudspeaker chirped through the silence: "Showtime in three minutes."

Standing at her workstation on the brightly lit stage alongside the two other contestants, Nadia Zannini trembled with nerves. The whole world would be watching soon. She felt out of place in the makeshift kitchen amid the antiquated tools like ovens, stoves, and aluminum cookware. Nervous sweat dampened the underarms of the ridiculous vintage housedress she had been forced to wear. Makeup bots whirred in the air inches from the women's faces, making last minute touchups to their powder, rouge, and lipstick.

"There's no getting out of it now," said Beverly Crick, her meek voice quivering and her eyes nearly bulging with fear. In her housedress, she looked like a failed sitcom mother from the 1960s, with her slight build and a worried look that seemed perpetually frozen on her face. She stooped down to the storage bin beneath her workstation, where she fumbled again with the stacks of pots and pans. A second later, Nadia heard her sobbing.

"There, there," Nadia said. She made her way over to Mrs. Crick's station, passing Mary Irons, the third and final contestant. Mary gripped the edges of her own workstation and stared coolly at the empty studio. Nadia made no effort to hide the contempt on her face. How could the woman stand there, stiff and emotionless, while their fellow sister was coming unglued? Clearly, they were all scared, but couldn't they show some compassion toward one another? She cupped Mrs. Crick's chin gently in her hand. "Pull it together, dear," she chided gently, "you'll ruin your makeup."

Mrs. Crick offered a wan smile and wiped at her eyes. "Better for the world to see us as we truly are," she said, sniffing. "As people. Not mindless toys for their amusement."

The studio doors abruptly opened. A stagehand entered, along with two men in plain clothes, followed closely by a pair of heavily armed soldiers. The men were the husbands of Mrs. Crick and Mrs. Irons. They gazed grimly at their wives on stage and then took their seats near the front of the audience. They sat silent as stones with their hands neatly folded in their laps. Mrs. Crick sniffed again, a fresh round of tears threatening to break loose. The soldiers stood close by with by their hands on their rifles, ready for anything.

Nadia gazed at the husbands. If Ross was still alive, he would be among them at this very moment. His death last year from the flu had been a cruel twist of fate, especially at such a young age—he was only 42. But there was no helping it, she supposed. The war had damaged the nation's economy, leaving many people malnourished and in poor health. Nadia only thanked God he had lived to meet their daughter, Rose. His death had come two weeks after her first birthday three years ago. As much as Nadia would have loved to have him alive, maybe it was better this way. Because then he would be here, and that was no place to be at all.

Then the audience streamed into the room. Every chair would soon fill, Nadia knew. After all, this was *American Housewife*. This show was special. Nothing topped it in the ratings, not even the *Olympics*. It had been that way ever since 2032 when the military had finally quelled the Female Rebellion.

The studio filled with chatter. Nadia overheard snippets of conversations about the events that had led them here today: the uprising, and how it had ended, the many lives lost, and how this annual tradition served to keep the peace across the land.

The houselights went down, and a throbbing dance beat began. Nadia's heart began to race. From far overhead, a man appeared on a shining, flying disc.

Rivers Fuqua, the host.

"Ready for another fantastic show, sweeties?" he asked over the loudspeaker.

"Yes!" The room called out in unison.

"Let's do it!" he sang out. The disc descended to the stage amid a flurry of flashing lights. The show's theme song echoed off the walls. Everyone clapped and cheered—except for the contestants and their husbands. When the disc had lowered completely, Rivers hopped off and strutted across the stage. He was a short, energetic man with spiky, silver hair and a mouthful of gleaming teeth. Spotlights lit up the contestants as he motioned for them to take their places behind the worktables. A camera-drone hummed overhead capturing their expressions and projecting them to a large overhead screen.

"Welcome to *American Housewife*," Rivers said, as he skipped off the disc. "You know the drill. Every summer, three mothers come together to compete in the ultimate cooking challenge."

Fireworks lit up the stage. A male and female figure emerged from behind purple curtains. The male, in a flowing, scarlet-colored robe, was the show's judge. The other was a female, brutishly built and wearing dark clothes and a white apron. Both wore masks filled with an amorphous, flowing gel that obscured their features. When the woman's head turned in her direction, Nadia felt herself holding her breath.

"Let's get started," Rivers shouted, "and may the best dish win!" The honk of the starting horn shook the studio, and a holographic timer on the stage wall started ticking down. The women grabbed shopping baskets and ran to the pantry. Mrs. Irons got there first, followed by Mrs. Crick. Nadia arrived last, struggling to catch her breath. She cursed herself silently for letting herself get so out of shape. The women snatched up their preferred ingredients and tossed them into their baskets.

Soon the studio filled with the sounds of cooking: the chopping of vegetables, the whirring of blender blades, and the scraping of mixes into pans. For Nadia, the tension was maddening. Rivers, ever the showman, kept the audience stoked by vamping across the stage. "Mrs. Irons," he said, cocking the microphone to his mouth, "would you mind telling the good people of America how you've prepared for the competition?"

Mrs. Irons kept her steely gaze on her mixing bowl. A camera-bot slid into position next to her. "I've spent every waking minute preparing for this," she said in a low, steady voice. "Read every cookbook money can buy. Memorized hundreds of recipes." A lock of brown hair shook loose from the scarf on her head, and she fingered it back into position. "Excuse me," she said sharply, "I really must concentrate."

"Touchy, touchy," Rivers chided. He covered the mike with his hands and whispered into her ear. "Remember sweetie, showmanship counts." He spun back toward the audience and lifted the mike to his lips. "Maybe the other contestants are in a better mood. Mrs. Zannini, you appear to be making a crostini? What's your inspiration?"

Nadia looked up at the audience, at all the faces staring back. She, too, read many books, memorized recipes, and practiced her cooking skills into the wee hours of the morning, but right now, she had no desire to discuss it. Looking out at the people who had come here to watch her struggle, she felt consumed by rage. It was getting difficult to think clearly. Her face was warm. A hot, sick feeling was spinning in her gut. She lowered her gaze to the cutting board: "I'm sorry, Mr. Fuqua. What was the question?"

"Such a showgirl," he said, rolling his eyes. "Let's see if our other contestant is feeling livelier. Mrs. Crick, same question."

Mrs. Crick tugged at the collar of her uncomfortable neckband with shaking hands. "Um, I'm here today for my c-country. W-we ladies need to be reminded that—"

"—a woman's place is in the kitchen!" the audience roared.

Mrs. Irons whacked her knife against her cutting board loudly, and an audible gasp filled the studio. Her fiery gaze turned to the audience. She opened her mouth as if to speak but was drowned out by a cacophony of boos.

Nadia caught her eye. "Tsk, tsk, sister," she said softly. "Is it really time for such things?"

Rivers stepped between the two of them. "Ladies," he said, covering the mike with one of his hands. "May I remind you that the treaty commands full compliance by **all** of our contestants?" The spotlight panned to the stage wings, where more soldiers waited. Mrs. Irons took a moment to regain her composure, and then the women got back to work.

At her workstation, Nadia had started to glisten under the spotlights. Her nerves were starting to fray. She tried to distract herself by humming while she whisked a bowl, but her voice quavered with fear. She began to work more slowly, measuring each ingredient twice, some even three times, before adding it to the mix. Poor Mrs. Crick wasn't doing much better. Her thin body was shaking from nerves, and she shattered one of her mixing bowls on the floor. An attendant brought her a new bowl along with a glass of water and a towel for her sweating face.

Soon the warm scents of rosemary and toasted breadcrumbs wafted through the studio. When the timer had counted down to the last few minutes, the women began plating their dishes and applying the finishing touches.

Then it was time for the tasting.

The judge lifted a forkful of each dish carefully into the mouth hole on his mask. His eyes closed as he chewed each bite slowly, and the amorphous shapes on his facemask twitched excitedly in response.

"Mrs. Irons," he said, after what seemed like an eternity to the contestants, "your salmon cakes are positively divine."

A smile curled its way into the corner of Mrs. Irons' lips.

"However, your plating lacks imagination. And Mrs. Zannini, your crostini has the right crunch, but I'm not getting nearly enough flavor. Mrs. Crick, the filling for your deviled eggs was rich and creamy, but the eggs were a trifle overcooked."

Rivers cut in to take the show to a commercial break. The contestants remained quiet on the stage, stealing glances around the set or into the audience, and waiting.

The cameras started rolling again, and the women were instructed to line up in front of the judge. They licked the corners of their lips, their hands folded plainly in front of them, except for Mrs. Crick, who wrung her hands together as if she were cleaning them. A slow, rolling drumbeat started over the loudspeakers and Rivers brought out a platter topped with a silver cloche. The camera-bot zoomed in to capture the moment, and Rivers flicked up the lid.

It was the salmon cakes.

"Mrs. Irons," the judge said, "your dish showed promise, but in the end the flaws overcame the goodness. For that reason, you've lost this round of *American Housewife*."

A wide door at the rear of the stage hissed opened, revealing a small room where three small children sat playing with toys. The broad-shouldered woman walked in. "No!" screamed Mrs. Irons when the woman yanked up a brown-haired girl by one of her arms. A rubber ball fell from the girl's hands as she was slung over the woman's shoulder. Nadia barely got a look at her daughter Rose before the door slid shut again.

One of the husbands shot out of his seat with a sharp cry, then quickly fainted. "Savage!" Mrs. Irons shrieked from the stage. "How could you?" She lunged for the brutish woman, but the soldiers subdued her.

The woman strapped the now-screaming toddler down on a large table. The attendants stepped forward to assist, wrapping the young girl's eyes with a blindfold. With one hand, the brutish woman selected a long, gleaming knife. Mrs. Irons shrieked over and over while the guards restrained her. A hush fell across the audience. A few of the younger spectators covered their faces. Most, however, leaned forward, their nostrils flaring, their eyes hungry. The camera-drone clicked and whirred, adjusting the focus of its lens.

Mrs. Crick's knees buckled, and she collapsed, sobbing. Nadia made the sign of the cross against her chest and muttered a silent prayer. Once again, she crossed the stage to comfort Mrs. Crick. The two women held each other, as if their embrace could somehow imbue them with the strength they needed to get through the rest of the show.

"Freshest meat in town," Rivers Fuqua said, winking diabolically into the camera. "Can't wait to see what the remaining contestants do in the entree round."

GIFTS

When he couldn't stand the buzzing in his head any longer, he swallowed the pill, a side-effect of which made him nervous. He ended up walking it off in the park where he heard the tinkling of a piano being played—"Für Elise," one of his favorites. Curious, he followed the sound into a clearing. There she sat at a public piano in a tight t-shirt, sunlight glinted against her short blonde hair, and she didn't say no when he scooted in beside her. They made music together, his nimble fingers darting around her clumsy ones. Soon the rhythm took over, like it always did, and his hands began to move faster as he improvised, lost in the mechanics of sound, of creation. It was a feeling close to godliness, he imagined, the unfolding notes and harmonies cascading off his fingers like sparkling flecks of water. When he looked down again, his fingers alone danced on the keyboard and she was turned towards him on the bench, staring. A crowd had gathered there in the dappled light and when he stopped at last, his chest heaving with exertion, they cheered and tossed dollars, begging for him to take a bow. He did and she took him by the hands. Her skin was soft like cream, and she smelled lovely, like lilacs in the summer. She kissed him on the fingers gently and strongly on the lips, and a fire raged inside of him for the first time, hotter than the glare of any concert spotlight. Shy though he was, he asked for her number. She scratched it out on a piece of paper and gave it to him. *Mary*, the name read.

That evening the buzzing returned so he took another pill and sat at his piano until his thoughts calmed. He barely slept, worrying whether or not to call her. He called her the next day, even though his voice was shaking from nerves, and asked her to meet him downtown for a soda. Surprisingly, she said yes. At a café on 59th street, they talked until the sun went down and he begged her to join him for a walk in the park. She straddled him on a bench, not far from the piano where they'd met, and she kissed his fingertips over and over again. "What else can you do with these?" she teased. Eagerly, he showed her. Her body wrapped tightly around his. "More," she moaned. The fire inside burned for her, but when he pulled out his member it was soft, another side effect of the pill. Working his fingers back into her shorts, he was surprised to find she'd gone cold. "Not tonight," she said. She left him listening to her staccato footsteps as they faded down the sidewalk. He didn't sleep that night either, plagued with thoughts about her, and when the buzzing returned in the morning, he decided enough was enough. He wouldn't be enslaved to the pills forever. No, it was time for him to stop.

Today.

For Mary.

The pill bottle on the nightstand was moved to a drawer, and while bugs buzzed in his brain he forgot about going to class, forgot about eating. His only thoughts were of her. But when he called his sweet Mary again, she didn't answer. So he called her again.

And again.

And again.

***

Her last boyfriend gave it to her hard and rough, just how she liked it; sometimes he called her names and struck her until she cried. But it was love, she knew. It was physical; she could *feel* it. Most guys didn't know how to give themselves that way. Last week he had dumped her because of her flirtatious manner. Upset and in need of attention, she put on her tightest t-shirt and went to the park. On a public piano, she played "Für Elise," the only piece she remembered from her years of piano class. When she saw the young man coming her way, she thought she recognized him from campus. Even though he was kind of awkward, she didn't mind when he sat beside her and started playing. She knew she was in the presence of an artist by the time he'd finished. He was slight of build, hardly a man at all, but she kissed him anyway, giggling inside when he asked for her number. She gave it to him, flirt that she was. He sounded so nervous when he called the next day she almost hung up the phone. She didn't, however. He might be an interesting toy for the evening. He had a childish kind of charm, she thought while he sipped on his soda, but there was something about the way he looked at her, about his eyes, something wild, maybe even dangerous. It didn't matter in the end, because on the park bench, when he couldn't get it up, she decided to call the whole thing off. He couldn't give her the hard love she needed. A guy like him couldn't give her anything at all.

And when the phone calls started the next day, she knew she had made the right decision. Though he was talented, something about him wasn't right. "Better watch that flirting," she scolded her reflection in the mirror, but the girl in the reflection was grinning.

***

Without his pills, the buzzing grew until it was like a jet engine in his brain, chewing up his thoughts and spitting out fragments. Why wouldn't she answer the goddamn phone? On the third day, when he learned she had changed her number, he smashed his own phone to pieces with his fists. He forgot about the outside world, watching with reddened eyes as the sun came up, went down, and came up again. He turned to the piano for solace, but his fingers only betrayed him, slapping impotently against the keys like lead weights. He could only think of her. His sweet Mary, who smelled like lilacs in the summer, who played "Für Elise" like a goddess, who had kissed his fingers over and over.

With a few clicks, it was easy to find out where she lived.

Now gaunt and haggard, he stood in his garage with his hand immersed in a bucket of ice. It had been there for almost an hour. He stared into the bucket. Once, those appendages had been so full of promise, dazzling his instructors with their exquisite dexterity, bringing audiences to their feet in applause. Now they were useless. He'd never be able to feel with them again, never again be able play passionately with them again. She had taken everything: his love of music, his ability to sleep, and his desire to take his meds. He turned on the saw and the spinning blade roared to life. For a moment, the tone of the machine's whirring pitch matched up with the buzzing in his head, and in that moment of clarity he wondered what she would do when the gift arrived.

***

By the time the package came, she'd forgotten about him completely. Winking at the mailman, she carried the small parcel to the kitchen. She sliced the tape with scissors and wondered why the paper was covered with tiny flecks of red paint. Lifting the lid of the shoebox, the fetid stench of spoiling flesh assaulted her, and a scream tore from her throat as she saw them lying there like five fallen soldiers on a bloody battlefield, grayish yellow against the delicate cellophane.

TREATS

At her kitchen counter, Bernice Jones stared down at the pumpkin she had just carved. Frankly, the damn thing gave her chills. There was something sinister about the triangle eyes glaring back at her, something dangerous lurking behind that jagged, crescent-moon grin.

Normally she went for more cartoonish faces at Halloween, but moments ago something had come over her. She had seized the knife powerfully, arthritis be damned, and her hands had taken on a life of their own, slicing quickly, almost manically, through the pumpkin's dense flesh. Well, scary or no, the jack-o-lantern would have to do. Trick-or-treaters would be arriving soon, and she hadn't time to carve another. She wiped the sticky pumpkin guts off her fingers, dropped a candle down into the hollowed-out belly, and carried the jack-o-lantern out to the porch. *Halloween,* she thought, *was there a gayer holiday in the whole world?*

Bare autumn branches made skeletal silhouettes against the sun's harvest glow. The leaves had fallen early this year due to the brutal summer—the driest since the heat wave of 1954. That year had been a doozy. She'd lost her husband, Harold, that same year. Hard to believe he'd been dead ten years already. A sudden gust of wind slammed the door shut, jerking her out of her thoughts. A handful of leaves whirled around in an invisible vortex. Odd. Up until then, the day had been still. But that was the weather for you. No matter what the muckety-mucks on TV said, you never knew what it was going to do.

Bernice eased the jack-o-lantern down onto the stoop and took a few minutes to survey her decorations. Tonight of all nights, everything had to be perfect. She readjusted the scarecrow in the rocking chair. Just this morning, she'd made it by stuffing some of Harold's old clothes with hay. It made her feel like part of him was with her again. She stroked the collar on the torn flannel shirt lovingly before stepping into the yard. There, she untangled the sheet ghosts flapping under the elm tree and fluffed the cotton spider webs blanketing the bushes. Real spiders gave her quite a fright, but the artificial webs added just the right touch of spooky drama.

Back in the kitchen, she filled a bowl with the best sweets she could find: Tootsie Rolls, Zagnuts, and Turkish toffees. Nothing cheap, like candy corn and butterscotch. Halloween wasn't the time to skimp on treats. The neighborhood expected a certain level of quality from Bernice, from the prize-winning pumpkins she grew in her garden, to the candy she handed out to the trick-or-treaters. Even parents from other neighborhoods carted in their children by the truckloads to ring her doorbell. Now, Thanksgiving was a fine holiday, full of warmth and spirit, and everybody loved Christmastime. But for full on magic and excitement, Halloween took the cake.

"It was a one-eyed, one-horned, flyin' purple people-eater," she sang as she smeared on green face paint and slipped into her costume. Then, after plopping a pointy hat on her head and lacing up her boots, she retired to the couch with a glass of sherry.

***

On the porch, the wind started up again.

It spun in tight circles, lapping up leaves and dust motes, taking on substance and density, forming into a dark cloud.

The cloud zigzagged close to the jack-o-lantern, hovered over it...

...and seeped into the open mouth.

Flames licked out of the face.

On Bernice Jones's porch, something woke up. Something powerful and evil and as old as the world.

The pumpkin moved. It started as a wobble. Then slowly, smoothly, the jack-o-lantern rotated to face the door, its eyes glowering with a palpable sense of malice.

The cloud billowed out of the pumpkin and oozed out into the lawn, working downward, seeping through layers of topsoil, leaving behind the still bodies of ants and grubs, their tiny hearts instantly frozen.

It continued on, into the roots of the elm tree.

The root cells felt a spurring to wakefulness as the cloud passed through. Though they hardly moved all year 'round—except for a few centimeters of growth now and again—they were moving now. They twitched and wiggled, pulled themselves taut, and strained furiously against the taproot. One by one, they tore loose. They squirmed through the earth, blind as worms, and popped up through the grass. Near the porch's edge, they gathered, and twisted around one another like snakes.

A fibrous shape started to form.

First, a torso. Then arms. Legs.

On the lawn, a gangly figure now stood. One of its feet tore loose from the earth, came down again. The other followed suit. The figure took several shaky steps and then stopped.

It was missing something.

Sinewy arms plucked the jack-o-lantern off the porch, set it down squarely on the shape's shoulders. The sigh of old magic lifted into the chilly air.

A neighbor came shuffling down the sidewalk. Doris Haversham gawked at Bernice's decorations, paying particular attention to the terrifying new creature with the pumpkin head on the porch. *Bernice has outdone herself again,* Doris's thought, before making a few mental notes for next year's decorations and hurrying home to tell her husband.

The creature watched, silent as a gravestone. Then it shuffled over to the scarecrow and worked its wiry fingers curiously over the moth-eaten fabric.

***

The doorbell rang at 6:15 p.m. Bernice yanked the door open and cackled her best witch's cackle but stopped suddenly. Her next-door neighbors, Brian and Judy Hanson, smiled back at her, dressed as a coal miner and a nurse, respectively. Their daughter, Lauren, stood close by, dressed sweetly as a princess in a ruffles and a tiara. She took a look at Bernice's face and shrieked before lunging behind her father. Bernice whisked off the hat. With some extra candy and a cookie from the cupboard, she coaxed the girl into smiling again.

It wasn't until the Hansons were waving goodbyes from the sidewalk that Bernice noticed the missing pumpkin. A pile of strewn hay marked where the scarecrow once sat. The clothes were gone, too. *Teenagers*, she thought. They were the worst part about Halloween. Already with the pranks, and it wasn't even night yet.

She was sweeping up the last bits of hay at dusk when an early group of trick-or-treaters came ambling down the sidewalk. There was just enough time to hurry back inside, put the hat back on, get into character.

When she opened the door again, she gave it to them good, waving her hands as if throwing a spell and cackling for all she was worth. One of the kids dropped his bag, he was running so hard.

It felt good to be back in the game.

Night came, bringing lots of trick-or-treaters. They came dressed as pirates and vampires, werewolves and skeletons; they came as cheerleaders, devils, and fairies. Pick-ups and station wagons cruised the streets, letting children out, picking them up again. Parents called out to the youngsters in the darkness, urging them not to run, to watch out, to say thank you, to not drop candy wrappers on the lawn.

But as Bernice's feet became sore inside the boots and the last pieces of candy rattled in the bowl, she'd knew she'd had enough. It would be nothing but older kids from now on. They always came later, rarely in costume and usually without a proper treat bag. She didn't have the patience for them, not after what they'd done earlier. She flicked off the porch light and lowered the shades.

The makeup came off easy.

***

At a quarter past nine, the doorbell rang again. Bernice sat on the couch, her belly warm from all the sherry. She crept to the door and gazed out through the frosted glass. A lone figure stood on the darkened porch.

"No more candy," she called through the door.

The figure shifted, listening. The doorbell rang again.

She swallowed hard. "Go away."

After what felt like a long time, the figure slunk off into the darkness.

She double-checked all the locks in the house.

When she picked up the sherry glass again, her hands were shaking.

***

Ring-ring.

The doorbell again.

On television, a talking head was rambling on about the Soviets on a news show, which meant it was almost 10:30. Bernice glanced at the blinds to make sure they were closed. She held her breath and tried to make her body small. Best to simply ignore the knock until they went away. Except, the sudden burst of light on the porch wouldn't let her.

It looked like...flames?

She hurried to the door, yanked it open.

Her doormat was on fire!

Rather, not her doormat, but a grocery bag sitting *on top* of her doormat. Flames chewed through the bag's paper walls. Blackened bits of ash broke free, did somersaults on the evening breeze.

This prank, she knew. Stamp out the fire and end up with a shoe covered in dog shit. They'd done the same thing to Doris Haversham down the road last summer. The little jerks were probably out there now, watching her. Well, she wouldn't give them the satisfaction. She snatched up the doormat and slapped it against the bag until the fire went out.

She smelled it in the smoke. The shit.

The laughter of teenage boys drifted out of the shadows. She heard sneakers hitting the blacktop as they ran away.

Good riddance to the no-goodniks.

When she returned with a bucket of water, she didn't feel angry anymore. She remembered being that age—too old to be trick-or-treating, too young for that mischievous streak to have worked its way out of your bones completely. She'd smashed her share of pumpkins back in the day, egged plenty of garages.

She was remembering those days still as she tucked herself into bed, and the sherry put her to sleep before long.

***

A dark veil fell over the neighborhood.

At the rear of Bernice's house, a spindly figure lurked in the shadows, barely visible except for two burning triangles of light that reflected in the glass of the kitchen door. Gnarled hands twisted the doorknob.

The door was locked.

But underneath the knob, a keyhole.

The fibrous tangle of roots that made up the hand separated. Several of the thinnest filaments lengthened and slipped into the hole. The lock clicked and the door creaked open. The figure lurched inside, its crude feet scuffling faintly on the kitchen floor.

It stopped in front of the sink. A knife gleamed in the moonlight, drying on a towel, a thin thread of pulp still clinging to the blade. The hand curled around the handle, picked it up.

Perhaps the knife would carve again soon.

***

Bernice tossed and turned in her sleep.

In her dreams, a shadowy monster pursued her. She ran, but the only place she could find to hide was a graveyard. She was ducking behind a tombstone when a thunderclap woke her. It took a moment for her eyes to adjust.

Candlelight flickered in her room. Strange. She hadn't lit a candle before going to bed.

The light was coming from her doorway, where a solitary figure stood.

Someone in a costume?

Was it a costume? The body seemed too thin to be human. Stranger, its limbs appeared to be made out of tangled vegetation. Vines, maybe? Natty clothes engulfed the intruder's gangly frame. Even weirder, he was wearing...a jack-o-lantern mask?

No, not a mask. She could see no head inside. Only a burning candle, the light of which filled the room with a baleful glow.

Those empty, burning eyes watched her.

This wasn't any jack-o-lantern. It was *her* jack-o-lantern.

The intruder's breathing rasped throughout the room—quick jagged bursts, like the panting of a tired dog. Something smelled foul, like rotting leaves. The intruder held a knife. *Her* knife. It was streaked with what appeared to be red paint.

What kind of creature was this?

She tried to scream, but the cry hung in her throat. She struggled to move, but her muscles resisted. Had the creature paralyzed her?

The phantom creature shambled forward, its movements stiff, as if in mockery of the human form.

Near the dresser, the thing paused. Something had caught its attention: A porcelain ghost figurine, one of Bernice's favorites. A hideous laughter filled the room, and the creature smashed the figurine against the wall. "Halloween," an ancient voice croaked. "Do you even know what that means?"

The voice echoed off the walls but also seemed to be coming from inside of her.

"Bernice Jones, do you know why pranks happen on Halloween?"

The creature knew her name, could read her thoughts. But what kind of a question was this? Halloween wasn't anything to think about. It was simply one of autumn's rituals, something you just did.

The phantom's voice continued: "On this night, the membrane between our worlds is thinnest, allowing *my* kind to visit to *your* world. It's nothing for one of us to slip inside the skin of a mortal and spread a little chaos. Those boys who started your fire earlier, what do you think got into them?"

It couldn't be true. Halloween was just a silly tradition, wasn't it?

"There's so much you don't know about Halloween, Bernice. But I'm going to teach you. Yes, Halloween is so much more than candy and costumes."

Hellish light filled the room as the eyes flashed brighter. Bernice saw movement near the footboard. A black finger, curled over. No, not a finger. A bristly, hairy leg. Seven more came into view, exactly like the first.

A tarantula! She hated spiders more than anything.

The tarantula's swollen body crept onto the sheets. It was massive, the size of her hand, horrible and black against the white of her comforter.

Another tarantula jumped on the bed, near her feet.

A flash of lightning illuminated the dark corners of the bedroom, revealing tarantulas everywhere—hundreds, maybe—writhing and quivering on the walls, leaping on the lampshades, streaking across the dresser.

Something scurried over her leg. Eight cruel eyes flashed in the darkness as the first spider scrabbled the length of her body, venom dripping from its fangs.

She closed her eyes to pray.

A bristly leg touched the bare skin of her throat.

With the force of her scream, the magic that held her let go. She bolted upright, flung the spider wildly away.

When the lighting flashed again, the spiders were gone.

But not the creature.

It was lumbering toward her.

She tore from the bed, pulling over the nightstand in hopes of slowing the creature down, and bolted for the hallway.

The creature's footsteps were right behind her as she hurried into the kitchen. The knife hissed through the air, the blade slicing through her nightgown, nicking her shoulder.

She reached the doorknob, but her hands shook too much to get the lock open. If she could get outside, call over to the Hansons, shout to anybody who could help her. Even the boys from earlier if they were still out there—

A fibrous hand came down over her mouth. She whirled around to face her intruder.

What the creature wanted was for her to follow it.

Though terror made her legs quiver, she trailed the lurching figure through the back door and into the yard. Wind howled through the treetops, whipping her nightgown around her frail body. In the rot-black sky, the waning moon struggled to shine through a mass of storm clouds like a cataract-covered eye.

The creature led her to the path at the rear of her property, past the dilapidated shed where she kept her tools, and into the garden. In the summers, she planted her pumpkins here, but the vines now were yellow and sagging. Any other time, she felt happy here. Tonight the place filled her with dread.

The creature jerked up an arm and pointed a warped finger toward the patch.

She felt herself stepping forward, soggy earth sucking at her cotton slippers.

The clouds shrank away, and the garden filled with silvery moonlight. She'd been wrong: some of the plants lived. Some even bore pumpkins. Strange, since she'd harvested them all days ago.

"Glory, no," she gasped.

Doris Haversham's vacant eyes stared out from a tangle of leaves, and her tongue lolled out over a sagging jaw. The skin at the neckline was torn, jagged. The heads of Brian and Judy Hanson had been stuffed under a nearby plant as well, next to their daughter's head. A tiara sparkled on her forehead.

There were heads under all the plants, dozens of them. Neighbors, most. People she'd known for years.

The wind picked up, bringing a sound that filled her heart with dread. At the garden's edge lay an expanse of woods, lush and green in the milder months but now soulless and haunting with the onset of autumn. Hundreds of wailing voices were coming from that direction, crying out in pain and misery. From the shadows, a host of dark entities emerged. She saw shades and specters and hairy beasts with blood-matted fur. There were armor-plated bugs with snapping claws, pulsing things with beaks, and oozing blobs with snaking tentacles. They descended from the sky as well—witches on broomsticks, shrieking banshees, and slobbering beasts with leathery wings.

Every horrible, make-believe monster she'd ever imagined was here, and they were coming for her.

Unable to bear the spectacle any longer, she fell to the earth and hid her face with her hands, but the sound of her crying was drowned out by the wailing horde and the hideous laughter of the pumpkin-thing.

***

The next morning, she woke in her bed, drenched in sweat. Pulling back the comforter, she found her nightgown spotted with mud. As she traced the dirty footprints to her back door, the memory of last night returned. She raced for the garden, bracing herself for what she would find.

Everything was as it should be. No heads peeked out from the pumpkin leaves. Not a solitary pumpkin grew on a vine.

She found her jack-o-lantern on the kitchen table, the candle inside burned to a nub. The knife lay on the counter, just where she'd left it. A fog settled in her brain, a confusion unlike anything she'd ever experienced. What was real, and what wasn't? Why was it so hard to tell the difference?

Soon after, Doris Haversham passed by on the sidewalk, whistling while she walked. Her head was still intact. Later, Brian Hanson honked on his way home from work. He seemed cheerful, had even waved.

She'd dreamed it, that was all. A nightmare. But one so vivid, she'd gotten out of bed, gone sleepwalking. Yes, that had to be it.

So she thought, until she found the knife-shaped rip in her nightclothes.

Something unholy *had* visited her. A terrible, malevolent force from another world had entered her home and delivered its message. A laugh started up deep inside her chest, starting as a mirthful giggle before growing into a maniacal shriek.

Halloween.

She'd been doing it wrong all this time.

***

A year passed.

On Halloween day, she got up early, just like always. She ate a good breakfast and spent a few hours making sure the decorations were in order. Then she opened her pantry, hauled out the bushel of apples. She'd been buying them all week to make sure she'd have plenty. It was Halloween, after all. Tonight, everything had to be perfect.

She strolled out to her shed, piled a stack of boxes under her chin and took them inside. The objects in the boxes, you had to handle carefully, but oh, how those sharp edges glittered when they caught the light.

A big night lay ahead. Time to get to work.

"It was a one-eyed, one-horned, flyin' purple people-eater," she sang, working the first of the razor blades meticulously into the yielding fruit flesh.

Yessirree, tonight would be one for the books.

THE LAST NIGHT AT THE BLACK BOAR TAVERN

People don't go to that part of town now. Not since The Black Boar Tavern closed. Now you've got hookers wandering the street, winos pissing in the alleys. People say the building itself is haunted. Kids don't walk past it on the sidewalk, they run. Vandals threw bricks through all the windows. The front of the building is covered in spray painted words, like *murder*, *devil*, and *die*.

Sometimes I'll drive out that way and stand in front of the tavern. If I close my eyes, I can remember what it felt like to work there during its heyday. The creak of the front door swinging open. Pop music spilling out into the street, the bass thumping, everyone bobbing their heads to the beat. All the laughter, the din of countless conversations. The hiss of beer bottles opening. The clink of glasses against the bar top. The heady mix of odors that mingled in the air: cigarette smoke, sour beer, bleach, the occasional funk of sweat.

That's how The Black Boar's story ended. But that's not how it began, at least for me. When I first started going there as a customer, the bar wasn't busy like that, not even close. It wasn't a trendy or even cool place to go. The building itself wasn't special; it was an old frame house built in the '40s that a developer converted into a bar. The white paint on the slats was dingy and peeling, and the porch overhang looked like it might cave in at any moment. Not exactly the kind of place that screams out "exciting". It was a sleepy kind of watering hole, kept barely alive by a trickle of drunks who called themselves regulars. I guess you could say the bar was just paddling along, a lot like I was back then. This was before I'd found any kind of purpose in my life. If you want to know the truth, I'd already pretty much given up at that point. There I was, twenty-two years old and already feeling like life wasn't worth living. Why should I give a damn about anything? In my mind, life had handed me a raw deal. I was skinny, awkward, and afraid of everything. With a name like Peter Ennis, I was doomed. "P. Ennis." Thanks, parents. My school life was a never-ending barrage of dick jokes. On top of that, my father was an abusive tyrant who had ground my self-esteem into the dust. My mother, God rest her soul, had taken her share of it too, but she'd been too insecure to leave him. When she died in high school, I couldn't wait for college to start. But then it did, and when my classes got tough, I bailed. I needed money to live on, but with mom gone, there was no way I was asking that monster for anything. For me, it was sink or swim.

What I did was *swim* in a lot of booze, which of course led me to *sink* even lower in life. At that point, I was spending most of my time in bars, so it only made sense that I work in one. I got a job as a doorman at a local sports bar. The work wasn't too hard. You sit on a stool at the door and check IDs and to keep out the young ones. I did this for a couple of years, bopping around from place to place. Either I'd get bored and quit or I'd get messy and fired. That's what led me to The Black Boar Tavern.

Except when I got there, Mr. Carmichael—that's the owner—he didn't want me working at the door. He took my chin in his fat fingers and turned my face from side to side. His muddy brown stare made me uncomfortable, and I could smell the onions from the cheeseburger he'd just wolfed down. "Nice looking kid like you needs to be inside, around the customers," he said, kind of prissily. Nice looking? Please. I looked like Screech from *Saved by the Bell*, and people took every opportunity to remind me. Everybody knew Mr. Carmichael was queer, that he got his kicks having boys around that he could lord power over. I played along because I needed the job. Anyway, he wanted me to be a barback. "A barback is basically a busboy for the bartender," is the way he sold it to me, like I didn't know that already from working in the business. I guess it was his way of making the job sound less shitty. A barback, what it basically boils down to, is the bartender's bitch. They take out his trash, keep his beers stocked, wash the glassware. They do the dirty work so the bartender can do his thing. And that thing is to make money for the bar.

Nobody made money for that bar like Jack Rollins.

All my good bartending tricks I learned from Jack during that last long, hot summer at The Black Boar Tavern.

For instance, it was Jack who showed me how to make the serving ice smaller before your shift. You pour a pitcher of hot water into your ice bin. The melted ice is smaller, so it makes more surface volume in the glass, leaving less room for mixers. Customers love it because the drink tastes stronger. Bar owners love it because it keeps costs down. You keep the bar owners happy, they let you get away with anything.

Jack was full of tricks like that.

But I'm getting ahead of myself.

Right away, you knew why Mr. Carmichael hired Jack off the street. Nobody had ever heard the name Jack Rollins before that day he came zooming into the parking lot on his motorcycle. I have to admit, he looked a little threatening with his goatee, tattoos, and those wiry muscles packed into a skintight t-shirt. He strutted into the bar with his chest puffed out like he owned the place. You could tell Mr. Carmichael was eating it up. His hands were fluttering about like horny butterflies, and he was licking his lips a lot. Anyway, Jack filled out a job application and that was that.

Even on Jack's first day of bartending, it was clear Mr. Carmichael knew what he was doing when he hired him. During Jack's first shift, this guy walks in off the street and orders a Long Island Tea. You could tell the guy was feeling a little out of place, just looking for something strong to take the edge off. Did Jack start making the drink right away? Not quite. First thing he does is get the customer chatting. "Hey," Jack would say. "What's your name? Where you from?"

Now, if you've never had a Long Island Tea, it's a drink with four different liquors. It's what bartenders call a "build" drink. You "build" it by pouring the ingredients on top of each other in the glass. Most bartenders make a Long Island Tea one booze at a time, as if they were laying bricks. Lift, pour, put the bottle back, repeat. Boring.

Not Jack. Jack's thick fingers curled around the slender necks of the bottles near his waist. Like an octopus with two bottles in each hand, he swung all four up at once—glug, glug, glug, glug—right into the glass. The bottles had barely made a soft clink as they slid home behind the rail before Jack had snatched the mixing gun out of its holder with one hand and bulls-eyed the glass full from six inches away. Almost too smooth to see, he holstered the mixing gun like a pistol and his hands flew in opposite sides to complete the stations: cherry, straw, boom! They plinked into the glass at the same time, smooth as you please.

Five seconds, I swear to God. He did it all without breaking eye contact with his customer and before the man could finish saying he was from Oklahoma.

At the other end of the bar, Garland paced back and forth with his face all pinched up. He was the kind of bartender who made your drink and then slunk back into the corner to play on his phone. Guess he could see where this was going.

That whole afternoon, people were lining up to get a drink from Jack. Garland hardly had any customers. It was kind of embarrassing.

That next day Garland didn't show up for his shift, and I don't blame him for that. A no-show gets you an automatic termination, so this meant his job there was toast. Which sucked that day, because we had customers waiting to get in even before we unlocked the doors. A lot of them were regulars from the day before, but some of them were now bringing friends along. The seats around the bar filled up fast, and some of the nearby tables, too. People were drawn to Jack. That's just how it was. They recognize a good bartender when they see one.

Mr. Carmichael was all red-faced about the Garland thing. "Ennis, you're behind the bar today," he spat, marching me from the stock room to the bar. Jack was wearing a black t-shirt that said *Yes today, Satan.* He glowered at us both with his arms folded tightly across his chest. My belly was all twisted up, like I'd swallowed shards of broken glass.

When Mr. Carmichael walked off, Jack said: "Keep out my way, you scrawny fuck."

The next eight hours, I worked harder than I think I ever had in my life. Jack was a blur of motion. He was throwing bottles into the air and catching them behind his back, all while he was serving drinks and ringing up tabs. It was something to see him work, let me tell you. He made it look so easy. I hustled behind him like a madman, washing his glassware, keeping him stocked, trying to anticipate his every move. More than once, he'd shoulder me rudely out of his way or shout at me to "Move!" All the while, the crowd kept building and building. Eventually, Jack was sweating like he was tired, and I could see him struggling to keep up. "You going to stand there, or you going to help?" he blurted out. I stepped in and ended up taking a few orders myself. Thank God it was mostly just opening beer and making simple drinks. When a lady asked for a Tom Collins, I had to ask Jack what it was. "Gin," he barked into my ear. "Sour. Splash of soda." That was the first drink I ever made.

At the end of the shift, after we'd turned in our money to Mr. Carmichael and taken the trash out, Jack counted his tips. "Here," he barked at me, flipping me a stack of bills bound by a rubber band. It was almost $400, more money than I'd ever made all at once in my life.

"Congratulations, kid," Mr. Carmichael said. "You're a bartender now."

Which is basically how I got the job.

That's when shit got weird.

***

The first strange thing that happened was during my first bartending shift. It was the next day and I was working at Garland's old station, right next to Jack's. The day was bright and sunny, but not hot. The windows were open, and people were relaxed and smiling, which meant the bar was making money. I was feeling pretty damn great to be behind the bar. It felt like things were coming together, maybe for the first time in my life. I was handing a Cape Cod to one of our regulars when someone tapped on my back. I'm telling you, I felt it distinctly, right above my left shoulder blade. Tap, tap, tap. I turned around thinking Jack would be standing there, but he was over at his station with his back turned toward me. It spooked me so bad that my whole body jerked, and I dropped that goddamn drink on the bar: The glass shattered and doused the customer in vodka and cranberry juice. Of course, that customer ended up being old Fred Skinner, one of our regulars. Skinner could get pretty mean when he was drunk. He jerked to his feet and called me a retard while I searched frantically for a towel. For a horrible second, all eyes were on me. Even Jack was staring at me like I was an idiot.

It freaked me out, but a few hours later I'd forgotten about it. I certainly didn't connect it to Jack.

Did I know Jack was into some dark shit? Honestly, I thought it was all an act at first. His love of heavy metal music. The satanic messages on his t-shirts. The pentagram that hung on a silver chain in the hollow of his throat. So what? Bartenders always want to look like the toughest guy in the room.

I never suspected anything until later that night. And even then, I wasn't sure what had happened.

Jack was taking a smoke break in the alley out back. Mr. Carmichael was working on next week's liquor order, so he sent me out to fetch him. It was dark and late. Jack was standing near the dumpster. He couldn't see me, but I could see him. And what I saw was he was talking to somebody. His voice was real low like he was trying to be quiet. At first, I thought he was maybe on his phone, but he wasn't. I was sure of that when I heard a second voice answering him. That voice wasn't coming from a phone; it was right next to Jack. It was a raspy voice, full of secrets and mystery, and it made my skin crawl. When I came up on Jack and called his name, nobody else was there.

"Fuck!" Jack jumped and dropped his cigarette. His nostrils were flaring with anger.

"Um, who you talking to?"

"The fuck you want, punk?"

The way he refused to answer me, it made the hairs on the back of my neck stand up. Like I'd caught him doing something he shouldn't be. Days later, I was still wondering if he was messing with me. Like, maybe he was putting on another voice to scare me. Or maybe he was schizophrenic, and I'd heard the voice of one of his other personalities. With a guy like Jack, either of those was possible.

You forget some of that stuff just because of how Jack was.

You forget some of that stuff because finally, people in town were talking about The Black Boar Tavern.

***

Jack was a good luck charm for that bar, despite what happened at the end. And yes, we'll get to that. First, you need to understand why I didn't just quit when things got weird.

By summer, Mr. Carmichael was making money. The bartenders were making money. Jack even started to warm up to me a little. Or I should say, it felt like he hated me less. I think it's because of how hard I worked to get better at the craft. When it came to bartending, Jack was a real role model. During our slow shifts, he'd start to teach me certain skills.

He told me a trick to help remember a customer's name. What you do is repeat it three times during their visit. "You say, 'Nice to meet you, Joe. Another beer, Joe? See you tomorrow, Joe.'" He tapped a finger against his right temple. "It's muscle memory, Slim. Each time you say that name, an invisible needle scratches a mark into your brain. Next time you see old Joe, his name will fly right out your mouth, just easy as you please."

I was in awe to be given a peek behind his curtain, but with my mouth hung open like that, I must have looked like a real moron. "These people come here for several reasons," he went on to explain. "Are they looking for a good drink? You bet. But also, they're here because they're bored. You got to keep them entertained, bro. Think of yourself not just as a bartender, but a magician. You got to put on a good show."

Jack would bring a new recipe to work with him every day. He'd make new versions of the classics. Melon margaritas. Hot pepper martinis. He'd make drinks with dirty names. Leg spreaders. Cocksuckers. Red-headed sluts. One day I asked him where he got his ideas. "The internet, dipshit," he said. "Everything's out there. You just have to know where to find it." He was hot and cold like that. It was embarrassing when he put me in my place, but what could I do? He spent hours dispensing his knowledge to me, and I soaked it all up like a sponge. Watching him create like that was magical—I felt like a young Jedi in training. Jack thought I was someone worth teaching, and that meant everything to me.

You ask me why I didn't say anything about Jack's strange tendencies? I was too busy worshiping him.

***

When you're a bartender, the rest of the world looks down on you. For instance, the teller at the bank stares down her nose when you bring in all that cash. Like it's dirty, somehow. Like you're dirty. It can really suck, but you get used to it.

"Get a real job," my dad said when I made the mistake of calling him on Father's Day. He doesn't understand how demanding bartending is. Standing on your feet all day. Putting up with drunks. All that reaching and bending and turning. Anyway, it didn't matter what he said. At that point, I was hooked on the money. Maybe more than that, I was hooked on the rush of it all.

Bartending gives you a feeling of power.

No matter where you've come from, or how bad you may feel about your rotten life, it all goes away during a busy shift. When the bar is slammed and everyone is looking to you for their drink, you don't have time to dwell on your own problems. It's all about your customers. For a few hours, you're their entire world. You're a star. Everyone wants to be your best friend.

There's really nothing like it.

**

This one afternoon before our shift, I was stocking my bar. That's the time to make sure you have all the supplies you'll need before you get busy, stuff like napkins, glassware, the like. There was just me and Jack in the bar. He was wiping his bottles down. I remember it vividly, even now. He picked up a liter of vodka. The sun was setting, and a shard of light shot through the window and lit up his face. His green eyes stared intently at the bottle.

He said, "Ever wonder why they're called spirits?"

"No," I said, which was the truth. What kind of dumb question was that? Nobody called them spirits any more. Nowadays we call it liquor, or hooch, or booze.

The bottle wasn't very full, maybe a quarter or so. He palmed the bottom of it and started swirling the liquor inside.

"When people in the old times discovered what fermented grains could do, they thought actual spirits were causing the intoxication. Like maybe the souls of fairies and nymphs that lived in the fields had gotten inside the liquid."

The vodka sloshed around lazily. There was something mesmerizing about the motion. He was speaking in a calm, controlled tone that was very soothing. Inside the bottle, the vodka was turning into a whirlpool.

He said, "They loved that feeling so much, they wanted to protect it."

There was mist inside the bottle. It started as a little puff of white, like a cloud. The more he swirled the vodka, the more the cloud turned into a cone. It was fluffy and white, like a whirlpool made out of cotton candy.

He said, "They would sacrifice animals to honor these spirits. They'd sprinkle their blood all over the wheat fields."

The whirlpool turned into a shape that was almost human. Female. The figure had a pale face and long, flowing hair that was kind of silvery. Her ears were pointed at the top. She had a long sloping chin. Her eyes were sockets filled with black. She wore a look of agony, of helplessness.

He said, "Sometimes, they even sacrificed their children."

He stopped spinning the bottle. The liquid splashed back down to the bottom. It was just vodka. The woman was gone.

"You got any children?" he asked.

I shook my head to clear it and stared at the bottle. The label had a picture of a woman in a potato field on it. I don't know why I'd never noticed it before.

"N-no," I said.

Next thing I knew, the door creaked open. A customer was walking in.

Jack's lips pulled back in a tight grin that made me uneasy. "Me either. At least, not anymore." Then he smiled a big welcoming smile to the customer, who took a stool on Jack's side of the bar. Jack started chatting him up like nothing had just happened, leaving me there with my mouth hanging open.

To this day, I still wonder what he meant by that.

***

No matter how strange some of those days were, you couldn't deny there was something profoundly interesting about Jack Rollins. He seemed like a guy who knew exactly what he wanted in life, and how to get it. Like I said, people were drawn to him. He was provocative, catlike, mysterious. I was drawn to him too. Not in a queer way, like fat old Mr. Carmichael. But in an admiring, reverential kind of way. Forget my father: Jack was a powerful male figure to look up to.

Working with Jack, I began to see what the rest of my life could look like. I started working out at home so I could look better: bicep curls, pushups, crunches, the works. I cut down on my drinking and started eating better. I started *feeling* better. I got some tight t-shirts to wear. Nothing with satanic stuff on it, that was Jack's thing. Mine were punk bands that I didn't even listen to. *The Misfits. The Ramones. Minor Threat.*

When Jack suggested I learn to start throwing and catching bottles, I felt like I couldn't say no. It was his idea for us to practice together. We'd come in early for our shifts and toss empty bottles back and forth at one another. Of course, Jack caught them all. Me, not so much. The bottle would slap awkwardly against my hand and then thump to the rubber mat below us. It didn't take long for Jack to lose patience. "Concentrate goddamit," he hissed at me. I got so scared of displeasing him that I took a bottle home to practice with after work. I practiced a few hours after my morning workout, just throwing them up in the air and catching them. Within a few weeks, I got pretty decent at it.

After that, we were a sight to behold. The customers would gawk at us all rosy-cheeked and happy, saying "Ooh!" and "Ahh!" and "Check it out!" No other bartenders in town could touch us. The bar business started to pick up. Even better, so did our tips. Mr. Carmichael thought it was pretty sweet. The fat fuck was able to work in a few more bags of fast food throughout the day. Man, it was disgusting to watch that bastard eat, but at least it kept him off our backs.

That's when Jack and I really hit our stride. Looking back, those were some good days. That's when I knew I wanted to do this job forever.

***

Jack taught me some cool things about bartending, but he taught me some shady things too.

Now, some bartenders, you can't trust at all. I knew this one guy who would pull a mean trick on customers he didn't like. He'd tell them he was out of fruit for their drinks. He'd run off to the cooler, carrying their drink with him as he went. As soon as the door shut, he'd drop his pants and plop his balls right into the glass, cold ice, and everything. Then he'd walk back out and serve them that same drink, smiling all the way. "Feels good," he'd tell me later. "Especially when you been busting your ass for hours."

Jack showed me how to handle a stubborn drunk who won't take the hint when you want to slow him down. Make his drink when he's not looking. You fill his glass up with coke or soda. Then you pour some booze into the tip of his straw. What he gets is what amounts to a thimble full of alcohol instead of the regular pour. When he sucks on that straw, that hit of booze dances across his tongue. He'll think his drink was made regular. You charge him eight dollars for the drink. Everyone's happy, the end.

Jack taught me how to drink booze behind the bar without getting caught. Most bartenders will sneak a shot by pouring it into a glass or cup, so what you do is make sure your boss doesn't see that. When they're not looking, you fill up a water bottle with vodka. The vodka looks like it belongs there, and you can take a big old swig right under your boss's nose. You get to drink for free and nobody's the wiser.

Then there's the Visine trick.

It was a trick Jack reserved for customers he disliked, mostly ugly girls or shitty tippers. He kept a bottle of Visine with him behind the bar. If he didn't like you, he'd squeeze a couple of drops into your glass. Visine is great for your eyes, but bad for your stomach—it's made with a chemical that's harmful if swallowed. Not everybody knows that. You get some Visine in your mouth, you've got the squirts for the rest of the day. Even the next day. Maybe longer.

I used it one time on Fred Skinner.

Like I said, Skinner was a mean drunk. One of the things he likes to do is bang his glass on the bar when he wants another drink. Ask any bartender, it's the most annoying sound in the whole goddamned world, next to somebody snapping their fingers at you. So that's what he did one day, started rapping his empty glass against the bar. Of course, he was having a conversation with some out-of-towner at the time, so he was really putting it on. It was his way of showing he had enough pull around the place to treat the help like shit. A real dick move, you know?

Rap, rap, rap.

"Service!" he said, when I finally looked over. His eyes were as bloodshot as his Cape Cod. He held his glass up and rattled around what little ice was left.

"Empty, Mr. Skinner?" I said, as nicely as I could, even though I was mad as hell. "My bad, sir. Let me get you another one."

"Damn right," he snapped, then went back to talking to the other customer. I started making his drink. When he looked away, I got Jack's Visine bottle and gave it a good squeeze.

That fool went on yammering on for about fifteen minutes after I set his drink down. Honestly, I got to thinking nothing was going to happen. Then all of a sudden, he got really quiet. He started kind of squirming around on his stool. Before you could say the words "toilet paper" he rushed off to the bathroom. When he came back, his skin was white as milk, and he wanted to tab out. Which was just fucking fine with me.

Later on, we found out he'd ended up in the hospital that night. Severe dehydration, brought on from a six-hour crapping spree. No, he didn't die, but it was a long time before we saw him again.

"How much did you use," Jack asked.

"Maybe a third of the bottle?"

"Shit! No wonder. Three drops, dude. Max." He slapped me on the back and laughed. "You could have killed that old geezer. Nice."

I was taken aback by the rush of warmth that flooded through my body, how good it felt to have his approval.

He must've really thought it was something because that night he invited me out for beers after work. We sat in a run-down lounge a few blocks down where the music was loud, and the drinks were strong and cheap. We sat at the bar, and we drank, and we flirted with waitresses until the place shut down. Then it was time for us to walk home. We were both pretty buzzed, and we didn't say much until we'd made it back to The Boar. The two of us were standing in the empty parking lot when he pointed at the building and said: "We've really turned this place around."

"We have," I agreed.

"That's cool. But man, we could take this so much further. What if I could show you a way to make more money than you ever had?"

"I'd say, 'Bring it on'."

"You won't like it."

"Why?" I chuckled a bit. "I gotta sacrifice somebody's kid or something?"

"Not quite," he said. "Here. Do what I do." He lifted up his right hand. Slowly, he bent the middle and ring fingers so that their tips were touching his palm. That left his other two fingers sticking straight up and his thumb poking out. He lifted his arm up so his palm was facing me.

It was a sign I'd seen before at concerts. "Fuck yeah," I said with a grin. "Rock and roll, man."

"Do it, Slim."

There was a sudden seriousness in his voice. I was getting tired of him bossing me around like that, but by that point the guy was my unofficial mentor in life, so I decided to humor him. Drunk like I was it took me a second to work my fingers into the position. When I got the fingers bent just right, I showed him.

"Good," he said. "Now hold it up like you're proud of it. Like I'm doing. No. Higher. Elbow out." I did like he showed me. We stood there staring at each other with our arms up like we were saluting a general or some shit. A moth flickered into a nearby bug catcher and fried.

"Now repeat after me," he said. He set his eyes firmly on mine. "Hail, Satan."

I snorted with laughter. "Dude, come on..."

"You chicken shit?" he said. He sounded irritated. "Say it, pussy. Hail, Satan."

"Hail, Satan," I said.

"Not like that. Like you mean it."

"Hail, Satan!" I shouted. "Hail, Satan!"

"That's it," he said, smiling. Already he was climbing on his bike. He revved the engine up started out of the parking lot. "See ya tomorrow, Slim."

I stood there feeling ridiculous for a moment, and then I stumbled back to my apartment. By the next morning, I'd forgotten all about the whole thing. Until the next night, when we had our busiest shift ever, by far. I shit you not, business was gangbusters. There was a line of people out the door all night. I made $1200 in just a few hours, more than I'd ever thought possible. Mr. Carmichael was over the moon.

At the end of the shift when I was counting out my tips, it all came back. *Hail, Satan.* We had both said it. Was there some kind of inherent power in those words? Was such a thing possible? Could it really be that easy?

So yeah, I did some bad, questionable things over the course of that summer. But don't judge me for it. Even on my worst day, nothing would ever compare to what Jack did on that last night at The Black Boar Tavern.

***

It was the last day of summer. The bar was packed almost every damn day leading up to that. Mr. Carmichael said our sales were higher than almost any other bar in neighborhood. But come tomorrow, all the college kids would be going back to their schools on their paths to becoming doctors, architects, and lawyers. As for me and Jack, it was our last big moneymaking night of the season, and we knew it. We were working our butts off.

But right around midnight, the tempo had slowed down. Even busy nights can only be so busy. Eventually, the party reaches a high point and people start going home. As far as work stress, it's all downhill from there. There were exactly 22 customers in the bar. With Mr. Carmichael, it was 23.

Right around one, Jack came back from his smoke break. He was pretty quiet for a few minutes and then he did something weird. He reached into his pocket and pulled out a silver chain. "Yours, kid," he said, slipping it over my neck. "You've earned it." I grinned when I realized it was just like the one he wore, with the pentagram and everything. The metal was cold on my skin, but I didn't mind. My breath kind of caught in my throat and I felt like I might cry, but there was no way in hell I was going to. Not in front of Jack Rollins.

"Thank you," I said, and I meant it.

"Don't thank me yet," he said. There was a twinge in his eyes I'd never seen before. Something was off about him. I'd be lying if I said I didn't feel scared.

Then what he did was call for everyone's attention. He clinked his bottle opener against the counter until everyone stopped what they were doing and looked over at him.

It was right at the stroke of midnight. I didn't realize it then, of course. I learned that a few days later when I read about it in the paper.

Jack stood right in the middle of the bar and closed his eyes. He stroked the pentagram with the fingers of both hands and seemed to be muttering something under his breath, although he was too far away for me to make out what he was saying. Then he opened his eyes and looked straight at me and said: "Nice working with you, bro."

Jack took a good swig of grain alcohol. If you don't know what grain alcohol is, it's strong stuff. The only people who ask for it are college kids. One shot will get you going. Two and you're seeing light tracers. Anyway, he reared his head back and then he flicked a lighter in front of his face and he spat.

The spray ignited. Fire leaped across the room. You've never seen anything like it. It was like a someone lit a blowtorch. For an incredible moment, every gleaming surface in that bar flashed brighter, every piece of glassware, every window, every mirror. If you were close enough, you could feel the heat on your face. There wasn't a head in that bar that didn't turn to look at what Jack was doing. As they watched him, you could see the fire reflected in their eyes.

Then something weird happened.

Every customer in that bar stopped what they were doing. It was like someone had zapped the room with a freeze ray. We're talking people in mid-conversation just pausing, their mouths still forming the words they were saying, beer bottles halfway to their lips. But that fireball didn't stop. That fireball was just burning and burning.

Besides Jack, I seemed to be the only person who could move. A chill passed through the air in the room. I turned and looked out at the crowd.

What I saw were these weird strands coming out of all the customers' heads. Just rising up out of their skulls and into the air. The strands were shimmering and ropy and milky-white. You ever see those old-time ghost photos? That ectoplasm that comes out of people who are supposed to be haunted? That's what it looked like. Whatever it was, those strands were being yanked out of the people, and they floated through the air over toward Jack.

Jack was waiting for those strands. His eyes rolled back in his head and his mouth hung open and the tendons in his neck bulged. One by one, he sucked those strands into his mouth. He kept sucking and sucking in with the biggest breath I'd ever seen a man take before, inhaling all of those strands into his lungs like he was hitting on a big old bong.

When it was over, the fire burned itself out. The customers started moving again.

The first scream came from a lady. She'd been holding a glass of wine. The glass dropped to the floor and shattered, and wine spread across the floor. What made her scream? Her husband had fallen to the ground, clutching his chest. His pupils were giant black orbs. He wasn't moving because he was dead.

A second after that, she dropped too.

Then, more screams rang out.

One after another, each one of those 22 customers started dropping like flies. Young ones. Old ones. Even Mr. Carmichael hit the floor. Boom, boom, boom.

It took me a second or two to realize what was going on. Looking out at those people dying like that, there was nothing I could do but start screaming myself.

I was still screaming when the cops arrived.

By the time they got there, Jack Rollins was gone.

22 customers lost their lives that night, all of them struck dead within seconds of each other. Nobody could ever explain it. The autopsy reports said they had died from massive heart attacks. That was the last night The Black Boar Tavern was open.

Of course, all eyes turned to me. The cops cuffed me and took me in for questioning. I told them the truth, that I hadn't done anything, that it had all been Jack. I spilled my guts and told them everything I knew about him, which at the end of the day, turned out not to be much. They let me go in the end. I think they understood they had another suspect to investigate, and his name was Jack Fucking Rollins.

***

The police searched through Mr. Carmichael's records. All of Jack's info was forged, of course. We'll never know who the real Jack Rollins was, or even if that was his real name.

THE LAST NIGHT AT THE BLACK BOAR TAVERN

Why was I spared? I'll never know. I think it's because, in the end, Jack respected me. Like maybe he saw something in me he recognized in himself. That's certainly not how we kicked off our relationship, but it sure seems like how things turned out at the end.

I know one thing for sure: I'll never see Jack again. He's probably moved to another town. I imagine he's already slinging drinks at another bar under a different name.

I've moved, too, to a sleepy little town about two hours away. It's a place where nobody really knows me. I got myself an apartment and a job at this hole-in-the-wall bar near downtown. The bar's name isn't important. But mine is, I suppose. They call me *Jack Bates* there. That's the name I put on my application. I like that name, Jack, the way it leaps off the tongue. There wasn't shit going on in this bar when I started working here. I guess you could say I'm waking the place up. The people don't quite know what to make of me yet. Me with my foul mouth and my t-shirts that say *Satan Lives* and *666*. Yeah, I gave up the rock & roll shirts. Jack was on to something; these devil shirts really get under people's skin.

Another thing Jack was right about is the internet. You can find anything you want there. Fake IDs. Talismans. Books on the occult. I ordered a bunch of those. They arrived in the mail, thick volumes with names like *The Satanic Bible. Necronomicon. The Lesser Keys of Solomon.* I've never been a big reader, but I tore into them like a hungry rat. That's where I learned about blood.

Blood does wonderful things.

Getting enough of it was easy. The sheep I found in a field on the outskirts of town. I crept up after dark just a few hours ago where a herd of them were sleeping together. The poor dumb beast never even saw me coming. One slit across its throat with a cleaver and a few moments of pitiful thrashing and then I'm gathering its blood in a bucket. An hour later, I'm back home.

Now, I'm sitting naked in the lotus position in my living room on a bunch of old blankets. I'm soaked head to toe in the sheep's blood and it's sticky on my skin and it's starting to smell. I accidentally licked a little off my lips, and it tastes like an old jar of pennies. But it's a small price to pay for what I'm about to receive.

Now I speak the invocation: "*I invoke thee, thou spiritual Sun. The terrible and invisible God, who dwellest in the void place of the spirit.*"

The table in front of me is covered with candles and crystals in the shape of a pentagram. Incense pours out of a cone, musky and sweet in my nose. I say the words over and over.

For a long time there is nothing.

Then it begins. A rush of warm air makes the hairs on my arm stand up. The curtains rustle although the windows are closed. A noxious smell hits me in the face, the stench of sulfur, the repellent odor of death. The temperature in the room goes up. There is a feeling of movement in the room and then I hear the unmistakable sound of hooves clacking onto the bare floor. A presence is there that was not a moment before.

I open my eyes.

And He is there.

There is no way to describe His countenance. How can one find the right words to describe Him? He is terrible and is beautiful, with qualities of human and animal alike. When his wrathful red eyes meet mine I tremble like an infant.

"*Peter,*" my new father says in a scratchy, croaking voice that's hauntingly familiar.

I am overcome by a wave of hideous, blinding fear; it is too much to bear. My legs buckle beneath me, and I fall as the old me dies. The blankets are wet; to my horror and shame I realize I have pissed myself. My body shakes. I moan in terror. I beg over and over for mercy. But the feeling lasts only for a moment and then it is gone.

When it passes, there is nothing but calm. My mind feels quiet, strong. Where once there was confusion, now there is a sense of purpose. Slowly, I find the strength to gaze fully upon my Master. When I do, it is a new man that rises from the tangled mess of blankets, who lifts his head proudly to the world for the first time. I reach out for Him. A powerful hand like a claw clamps tightly around my own.

Then the lessons begin.

THE GROUCH

You're not supposed to argue when a customer insults you, even if they act like a monster. It's the number one rule for retail workers during the holidays. Everyone's emotions are too revved up, you're supposed to keep situations from escalating out of control. Sales are king. Suck it up, Jasper Crumpledash thought when the ten-year-old got up in his face.

Overhead, Bing Crosby was wailing about chestnuts roasting on an open fire for the third time that day. Year after year, the endless loop of seasonal holiday carols was the worst thing about the holidays.

Scratch that. Crappy customers like the little tyrant in front of him definitely took the cake. "Young man," he said with a sigh. "As I've kindly explained to you twice already, Dirk Actionface is *the* hot toy of the season." He glanced around the store for the kid's mother. "Nobody knew the movie would be a hit. Demand for the toy simply exceeded expectations."

The kid folded his arms haughtily in front of his chest. It was the kind of gesture he'd probably learned from his father; most likely a rich corporate executive, judging from the kid's flashy clothes. "I'll ask you again," the kid snorted. "What kind of piece-of-shit manager runs out of Dirk Actionface toys at Christmas?"

When you're working long retail hours during the holidays, they tell you to keep a water bottle under the register to stay hydrated. They tell you to avoid heavy foods and alcohol before bedtime. You're supposed to get eight hours of sleep each night to minimize stress. Since you're standing so much, they tell you to put cushy inserts in your shoes. If a customer steals something, you're not supposed to chase them. And, most importantly, for the love of God, don't argue if a customer insults you.

Jasper figured the rule applied to his adult customers, but did it still count when the insult came from a kid? The kid was like, half a real person, right? For Christ's sake, he barely reached Jasper's elbows.

The kid stepped out of the line and came around the register, barging into Jasper's personal space. "I guess what you're telling me is, you're not only a piece of shit, you're a lousy manager, too?"

Jasper felt his nerves fraying. He'd worked fourteen days in a row, his lower back felt like a nuclear bomb going off and he hadn't had a restroom break in six hours. And now this? He shrugged, tinkling the bell on the green elf hat the owner made him wear. It was Christmas Eve. If he could only keep his sanity a few more hours, he would have tomorrow off. After that, things would go back to normal. The stressed-out shoppers wouldn't be nearly as stressed out, and he'd have all that overtime pay to go toward child support.

Jasper lifted his gaze over the kid's head and saw the crowd in the mall, or "the Maul" as he not-so-affectionately thought of it. It surged there in a swarm of movement, all those hot bodies threatening to fill the cramped space, the cacophony of voices uniting like the murmur of a hungry beast. For a second it looked to him like a huge, ravenous organism with a thousand separate heads, a capitalistic entity consumed by one overwhelming need: the urge to buy *more*. He blinked away the impression, fighting back the urge to flee for the exit.

The kid's voice pulled him back to reality. "Don't ignore me. I'm a potential customer and I'm talking to you, you big loser."

The shoppers clutching their toys in line all seemed to hold their breaths, drawn to the confrontation like flies on a hunk of rotting meat. Jasper's hands trembled with anger, so he lowered them below the register. "May I help the next customer?" he said.

"Ignore *this*." The kid made a hocking sound in his throat. A second later, a loogie splattered against Jasper's blue Toys Ahoy smock. It clung there in a greenish-white glob like some kind of alien amoeba.

Jasper whirled to face the kid, his mouth twisting into a sneer. "Enough!" he barked, his voice cutting through the tension like a whip. Without thinking, he placed his palm in the center of the kid's chest and shoved. The crowd of onlookers gasped as the kid staggered into a display of stacked toy cars. The toys went flying in every direction.

"Jasper!" The store owner came running from the back of the store, where she'd been working with customers. When she saw the kid on his rump amid a pile of strewn boxes, she clopped her hands against her powdered cheeks. "My word!" she said, helping the kid to his feet. "Are you okay?"

The kid got up, his beady eyes flashing. "My dad's gonna sue your pants off."

"He should," a mom in the line said as she pulled her young daughter close to her side. "We all saw what happened."

Marcy turned to Jasper, her angular bob stuck like a helmet against her head, as if she'd shellacked it with a whole bottle of finishing spray. With a blond tuft sprouting from the back of her head, she looked like a cockatoo with an attitude. "What's gotten into you?"

Jasper held out his smock as evidence. "Christmas! Is it any reason for these people to act like animals? No respect for the workers, no common decency. No concern for anyone but themselves."

"Jasper, your voice—"

Jasper felt like a pressure cooker about to explode, and the only thing that eased some of the pressure were the words flying out of his mouth. "It's all so stupid! All this shopping, all the talk about Santa. Why, in just a few years, they'll find out he's a big, fat lie."

Another gasp rose up from the onlookers. The girl looked up at her mother and started to cry.

"Who does he think he is?" the mother asked.

Someone else said: "Look at that snarl on his face."

Marcy stepped behind the register, her eyebrows knitted together in a vee. She took a long look at him, her eyes darting from his ear to his eyes to his other ear. "Go home and get some rest," she commanded.

This wasn't the time of year to lose any hours of pay. "My shift ends at six."

Marcy puffed out her chest in a show of superiority. "Then, you leave me no choice. You're fired, Jasper."

"Fine!" Jasper tore off his hat, pulled the smock over his head. "Eight years with this company gone, just like that." He chunked the clothes into the wastebasket. To the kid, he shouted: "Hope you're happy." Then he pulled his coat from under the register and stomped away toward the mall.

He had nearly left the toy store when Marcy called back. "Oh, and Jasper?"

He whirled to face her, his vision nearly blurred with rage.

"Get yourself to a doctor," she said. "You're looking a little green."

"*You're looking a little green.*" Jasper mocked Marcy in a singsong voice as he slammed open the mall's exit doors. The chill in the early evening air hardly got his attention. What did get his attention was the sound of a ringing a bell. Huddled in a threadbare coat, a Salvation Army worker was taking donations. She grinned at him, revealing several missing teeth. "Merry Chrithmtath," she called out.

"Is it?" he snapped.

The woman gaped at him. "Yeesh," she said. "What a gr—"

"A grouch?" he interrupted. It wasn't the first time he'd heard it. Linda called him the same thing every year at Christmastime, or at least she had when she still spoke to him.

"Not where I was going, but yeah."

He dismissed the woman with the wave of his hand and continued on.

A few seconds later, it hit him. She'd only been doing her job. He'd done to her what the kid had done to him. Now he felt like an ass.

Christmas was the absolute worst, he thought. It had been that way ever since he was a kid. Growing up the only child to poor parents, there was never enough money to do Christmas properly. His parents never decorated the trailer, could never afford a tree. Gifts? Please. One year, he'd gotten a bar of soap. Another year, Santa left him a Twinkie. After returning to school from holiday break, he stewed with envy as his classmates paraded around in their new coats and boots, brought their shiny toys to show and tell.

A stiff drink or three, that's what he needed. The embrace of liquid oblivion. Hopefully, he'd sleep well into tomorrow. When he finally stumbled out of bed in the afternoon, Christmas would almost be over.

***

On his wedding night, Jasper had downed too many cocktails, leading to a daylong hangover that nearly cost him his marriage. Once, a stomach bug had him spewing fluids from both ends at the same time. When he was six, he'd been rushed to the hospital to have his stomach pumped after eating an entire bottle of Flintstone's vitamins because they tasted like candy.

When people say you're looking a little green, they never really mean it. What they mean to say is, you're not looking well. All those times Jasper had been ill, he'd never turned another color besides pale. Certainly, he'd never turned any color even remotely resembling green.

Now, peering at his reflection in the bathroom mirror, he knew Marcy had understated things. He was more than just a "little" green.

His skin had turned a sickly greenish hue all over. He looked like pea soup gone bad, or like the snot in the kid's loogie. He stuck out his tongue. Green. He pulled down his eyelids. The green was there too, in his eyeballs and in the jumble of meat just beneath. He tugged off his clothes and looked at his naked body. Belly. Legs. Crotch. All that same sickening shade of green. He felt a little off, too. A doozy of a headache was kicking up in the middle of his forehead. Eyes squinted against the pain, he staggered out to the living room to huddle on the couch.

He lost track of time sitting in his dimly lit apartment, clutching his hands against his skull like he was trying to hold his life together. He'd seen this kind of thing before. One of his only friends at the mall was a guy named Larry who ran the hot dog kiosk. Larry had gotten so sick, he'd ended up quitting his job. When Jasper visited him at the hospital, Larry informed him of the cancer that was rotting him from the inside out. Jaundice turned him yellow from his skin to his nails to his eyeballs. He looked like he'd been dipped in the same mustard he squirted on his Chicago Dogs. That was the last time Jasper saw him. A month later, Larry was worm food.

Well, whatever the coloring was, it would have to wait. The doctors were all closed for the holiday. If he was still green in the morning, he would try to find an emergency clinic. Other than the headache, he didn't feel too awful. Just really pissed off. "Fricking Christmas," he said. "What else can go wrong?"

As if in answer, his neighbor's Christmas lights came on. Framing the neighbor's front door, the string of colorful lights twinkled brightly, cutting into the gloom of his living room. They flashed on and off, sparkling in an array of colors through his open blinds— red, green, blue, white.

With every flash, the headache grew. Jasper swallowed hard, doing his best to ignore the pain. His attention fell on a framed photo on the coffee table. Linda and the boys. When the lights flashed off, he could see his family perfectly. When they flashed on, everything was lost in a depressing garish glare.

How fitting the photo would catch his eye, on *this* of all nights. Tomorrow marked a year since "the incident." That's when Linda had gotten so mad at him, she'd kicked him out of the house. Because her job was taking her overseas for the entire month of December, and she'd given him strict orders to show the boys a good holiday.

"It's not *their* fault you hate Christmas," she'd told him at the airport. "They're children, Jasper. Let them have their fun."

He'd pecked her on the cheek, waved her goodbye, told her of course.

And hadn't he done everything she'd asked? He'd put up the tree, decorated the house, bought them presents. They'd had a great Christmas, he'd thought. He'd even made them a wonderful holiday lunch with roast beef, dressing, and all the trimmings. His fatal mistake, according to Linda, had taken place after lunch.

"Alright, boys," he'd said, clearing the dining room table. "Time to pack it all up."

"Pack what up?" Marcus asked, his eyes glazed over in a dreamy pecan pie haze.

"The tree, the decorations, all of it."

Jasper probably should have known he'd stepped in some kind of trouble, by the way Bobby started bawling. Bobby being the youngest, Jasper thought the boy was simply being dramatic. Whatever the reason for the outburst, by one' clock anything related to Christmas was back in the attic. Jasper enjoyed the rest of that day watching football with a can of beer in his hand.

On the couch, the headache grew. It felt like a spider had planted an egg right inside his head, tucked it away in a shiny gray groove of brain tissue right between his cerebrum and cerebellum.

He tried to focus on the photo. Losing Helen hadn't been the worst; they'd never truly seen eye to eye on anything. But losing his boys had hurt. Yet another knife in the back, courtesy of everyone's favorite freaking holiday.

The lights flashed. His head pounded. The lights, the lights, the godforsaken lights. They were the essence of Christmas. The lights seemed to symbolize everything wrong in his life. Because of Christmas, he'd lost his job, his family. Now even his health was in question.

Flash off. Everything was fine.

Flash on. Christmas crapped on everything.

The lights flashed. Jasper writhed on the couch in a blinding flurry of pain, both physical and emotional. His chest felt like it might burst open with rage. In his head, the egg was expanding. He imagined it there, a fuzzy yellow sac clinging to his cranial matter like a tiny unwanted testicle. With every passing second, the sac was probably growing like those time-lapse videos from biology class, swelling and expanding as the babies inside clambered against each other in the dizzying frenzy of fresh life, growing and growing in that crowded space, until finally—

The egg popped open.

Jasper tumbled to the floor, unable to bear the pain any longer. Convulsing, gasping, foaming at the mouth, his body jerked about in a tarantella of movement.

Now the pain was everywhere. His head, his limbs and torso all stretched and contorted, the cracking of his joints like dry twigs snapping under a heavy boot. His nose elongated into a snout, the tip of which was a dull olive green. A flurry of sensations raced through his skin, from irritation to itching to burning, and then a thick pelt of emerald hairs sprouted from every pore, covering him in a coating of shaggy fur. He reached to the ceiling as if imploring help from the heavens above, but God would not answer. Instead of hands, he saw two monstrous paws at the ends of his arms, the tips of each digit sharp like tiny green knives. The corners of his mouth twisted painfully up, up, up as if being yanked toward his ears by invisible fingers. He tried to call out in pain, but the sound that came out was a guttural snarl that reeked like garlic and decay.

He gaped in the mirror, his eyes transfixed in horror, in wonder. His body, once meager and lean, was now decidedly pear-shaped with a bloated green belly protruding under his skinny green chest. Baggy folds extended down his jowls like the face of a bulldog. Bushy brows rose from his forehead like horns, giving him the menace of a Vaudevillian stage villain. And everywhere he looked, that thick coat of fur which gathered in shaggy patches on the top of his head, on his crotch and in circles around his neck, wrists and ankles.

The impossible had happened, but it happened quick, at least. Jasper had hated Christmas so much, he'd turned into a beast.

With spiders scrambling his thoughts, the beast glowered at his reflection. Had it hurt? Yes, it had. Like one giant ouch. But he'd fought through the pain to let out his Grouch.

The Grouch trampled out into Jasper's living room, where he was stunned momentarily by the neighbor's flashing lights. He stared at them through the window, a garland of brilliant color framing the door to apartment 112. *Flash, flash, flash.* The more they flashed, the more he despised them.

Maybe there was something he could do about it.

On the patio, he ripped the lights down. Still they flashed.

The Grouch snarled. Another yank brought them flying from their socket. The cord dangled from his claws, dark and impotent. They felt flimsy in his clutches, cheaply-made products designed for superficial fools. Rage filled him at very idea of them. He hurled them to the ground, pulverized them under his feet with a clomp, whomp, stomp.

When he was finished, the Grouch stood amid the tangle of wires and plastic. He grinned a slow grin, the edges of his mouth curling up almost to his eyes. What was this new feeling blooming inside of his chest? Instead of rage, the Grouch felt giddy, luminous, quite simply, the best.

Then as soon as he had felt it, the feeling started to fade. He wanted to feel more of it. He turned toward town, where his gaze fell upon the points of thousands of twinkling lights.

The Grouch walked toward the lights with lumbering footsteps, following nothing more than the lights, his instincts. He was unaware that a glimmer of Jasper's intellect still burned in his brain. Like a mad puppeteer, Jasper stoked the fire of rage burning inside the beast's chest with his thoughts. *Was there a worse day in the world?* Jasper goaded the beast. *The way the entitled kids of today expect presents. How everyone works their asses off to buy that perfect toy for their children, only to find it tossed away two weeks later, broken and forgotten. How you're forced to be polite to relatives you spend the rest of the year trying to avoid. The way corporate profits soar, while children in poor nations starve to death.*

***

When you don't want people to see you at night, you're supposed to wear dark clothing. You want to move with ninja-like stealth. You're supposed know your route like the back of your hand, be aware of all the shadowy places you can duck into if someone's coming.

The Grouch did none of these things, yet remarkably not one person saw him as he trekked across town.

Eventually, he stopped to peep through a random window. The house was one of those new ones, all square shapes and big bright windows. The den was awash with holiday décor, a veritable sanctuary of cheer and light. The Grouch watched for signs of inhabitants, but the house appeared to be empty. This time of night, the family would be at church or a holiday party. A moment later, he stood inside the foyer, bits of glass from the shattered door clinging to his shaggy feet.

On the TV, a video game had been paused in the middle of play. Rifle held high, Dirk Actionface was frozen in the middle of an attack, poised to clobber an armada of rampaging aliens. The Grouch snarled at the sight of the action hero. Then he stomped on the game's controls and entered the living room.

The Christmas tree loomed before him, its many baubles mirroring the reflection of his gnarled grin. With a flick of his long, taloned fingers, he plucked off the ornaments, crushing them into bits of glass and dust in his shaggy paw. This debris, he hurled above his head until particles rained down on him like a snow globe, the very air now alive and shimmering. Below the tree, his gaze hovered over a carefully wrapped gift—a bright red box with a golden ribbon tied in a perfect bow. The Grouch grinned. With the gnash of his yellow teeth, he tore the ribbon into shreds, before ripping into the paper with his claws.

His grin twisted wider when he lifted the item to his face. "Ho, ho," he snarled, "what have we here? It's the most desired toy for Christmas this year!"

Oh, but the plastic action figure stirred his loathing. Dirk Actionface with his handsome, chiseled jaw. That all-knowing smirk, so full of confidence, of mischief. It made the Grouch sick. Bristling with rage, he twisted the head off and hurled it against the room. He slashed off the tactical vest and camouflage pants. One by one, Dirk's arms and legs came off with a crack, until a naked, headless torso remained. This, the Grouch smashed against the wall until it was broken in pieces.

With every act of destruction, a wild sense of glee filled the Grouch's heart. At the hearth, he plunged his paws into the hanging stockings, their bellies full and bulging. He rummaged through them all, pulling out candies and trinkets, only to grind them into the carpet under his feet. On the mantle, a ceramic Santa sat on his sleigh. The Grouch spat on Santa's face, then launched the figurine into the fireplace.

The room was chaos now, a Christmas undone. A barrage of thoughts ran through the Grouch's head. It felt good to destroy, it felt good to crush. Ruining Christmas really brought on a rush. Shoulders heaving, he stood amidst the wreckage and laughed, a thunderous and guttural sound that boomed across the entire house.

The joy only lasted a moment, though, because quickly the feeling faded. The Grouch's jagged breath quickened, and his eyes flared with renewed hunger.

This house is ruined, but this house can't be all. I know, he thought. I'll head to the mall. For holiday décor, it's got quite the stash. Filled with hundreds of items to bash, crash and smash.

The Grouch headed back to the foyer. Maneuvering through the hole in the glass door, he stepped out onto the porch, where he was bathed in a flurry of red and blue lights.

"Freeze!" a man's voice shouted. Five figures stood in a tense line in front of several police cars, weapons raised.

"Holy shit," another said. "Dude's naked as a jaybird."

"Hands up, weirdo," the first voice said.

The lights flashed into the Grouch's rage-filled eyes, erratic and sharp. He tilted his head. What were these lights? They didn't twinkle like the lights on the strings, but still he hated them, oh yes, how he hated these things. He wanted to smash his fists into them, he wanted to watch them shatter. He wanted to hear the pieces fall to the ground in a clatter.

Arms outstretched and claws grasping, the Grouch surged forward with a beastly roar. Two gunshots rang into the night. The Grouch fell to the ground, clutching at the gaping wounds on his chest.

He was aware of the commotion as the police drew nearer, their guns pointed at his head. Another car approached, its bright lights pulling into the driveway. A car door opened, and a man get out and joined the officers.

Dressed in a red sweater and dinner jacket, the man had the air of a wealthy and powerful executive, or maybe a senator. "This is my house, officers," he said. "What's the situation?" A kid got out of the car, rushed over to his father's side.

"Responding to an intrusion alarm. Caught this sucker trying to get away."

The man and the kid stepped closer to get a better look.

"Careful," the officers warned. "Could be dangerous."

The Grouch looked up at the faces staring down at him. He recognized one of them as kid from the store. The Grouch hid his face behind his outstretched paws. "Don't...look at me," he gasped. "It wouldn't be... rightful. I'm... warning you, now. I'm truly... quite...frightful."

"The fuck's he saying?" an officer said.

"Holy shit," the kid said. "It's the manager from Toys Ahoy."

"He's completely deluded," another officer said. "Any idea why he's in your house naked?"

The kid shook his head.

"Must be some kind of pervert," his dad offered.

"A shitty manager," the kid said. "And a pervert, too. What a loser."

When you're dying, they tell you your entire life flashes before your eyes like a movie on fast forward. They tell you your spirit rises up and when you look down, you see your body lying there. They tell you a golden light appears, and you'll float toward it, an eternity of warmth and love waiting for you on the other side.

Jasper experienced none of these things. He only felt stupid and alone as the cold December night eased his torment at last.

STORY NOTES

I've always been fascinated with the story notes at the end of collections. I love stepping into the writer's head, knowing what inspired the tales I was reading, getting a glimpse of all the ingredients that went into the stew. This collection has 30 entries, so I won't comment on every single piece. But I'd love to share some insights on a just a few, if you'd graciously lend me your time.

THE WEEDS AND THE WILDNESS YET

There are times that the act of writing surprises me, where something appears suddenly on the page, something so strange, bizarre, or completely unexpected, that it ignites a deep curiosity to find out more. It doesn't happen every time I write, but when it does, it's such a rush that words can't describe it. Such is the case with this story. I frequently do freewriting exercises, where I take a random topic and let 'er rip on the keyboard for a certain amount of time, capturing everything that flows out of my head without editing or critiquing the output. During this particular exercise, the topic was "growing like a weed". A few minutes in, I saw this scenario in my head: while working in his garden, a widowed man finds a strange plant that resembles his recently deceased wife. Like, what? I was hooked. Now, I'm a huge fan of plant monsters, just ask anyone. Alan Moore's *Swamp Thing* holds a special place in my heart, as do the vegetal aliens in *Invasion of the Body Snatchers*—the '78 version, not those other cheesy rip-offs. This story pays homage to both, hopefully. Anyway, once I had the idea in my head, the characters of Charlie,

Mildred, and poor, doomed Sidney quickly materialized, in a tale of a married couple with a loving bond that even death itself can't sever.

GHOSTS ON DRUGS

In the interests of my continued mental self-care, I should probably refrain from talking too much about my past in these pages. However, I've never been too secretive about some of the dark roads I've hurtled recklessly down in my day. I've had some pretty bleak years. Honestly, it's a miracle I survived some of the craziness I put myself through. The pain of those experiences notwithstanding, I'm thankful for every situation I've been through, because it's led me to where I am today, and that's a pretty good place to be. So, yeah, I went to hell and back, bought the t-shirt, and came through it with lots of good story material. That's not to say this story is autobiographical; it's not. The main character isn't me, not really. But pieces of him are me. And pieces of him are not. Which are which, you ask? I'll never tell. That's what makes writing so much fun. By the way, the spooky folks over at No Sleep podcast published this tale in audio format. You can find it on their website—just go there and search for the "The New Decayed episode 1", or by my name. It's a pretty fun listen, hope you enjoy.

IN THE NIGHT, A WHISPER

I'm blessed to have a very loving family, among them a brother-in-law, who, along with his wife, always come to Christmas bearing the coolest gifts. One year I unwrapped "The Beauty of Horror: A Gore-geous Coloring Book." I love cracking that book open for writing prompts: sometimes I'll open it to a random page and write whatever I see. That's where I first saw the girl in the devil costume who immediately won a place in my heart. I couldn't stop wondering who she was, what she was doing out in those spooky woods alone. She had a story to tell, obviously, and it seemed that I was chosen as the person to tell it. The boy, of course, is partly me, filled with a wide-eyed love for Halloween, which is the best holiday in the world. (Yes, I'll die on that hill.) So, why are the sections numbered? At that time, I had just discovered the works of Robert Coover, a brilliant writer who creates these captivating experimental stories that blend reality with illusion. Coover often numbers his sections in a similar manner, since his stories jump around in time so much. While his work isn't outright horror, the outcomes of some of his stories are truly unsettling. The first short story of his I read was "The Babysitter," and, wow, I was immediate hooked. I highly recommend his work, if you're into this dark fiction thing, which you seem to be since you've purchased this book. Anyway, I suppose his writing voice got into my head, as so often happens when I read new authors, so this story is sort of me, paying tribute to Coover, in my amateurish, awestruck, hero-worshippy kind of way.

EVIL INC. (OR HOW TO SUCCEED AT BUSINESS WITHOUT REALLY DYING)

I didn't start writing professionally until later in life, which means I've had some interesting jobs over the years. I've been a waiter, a salesman, a secretary, a pizza maker, a janitor, and a bartender. And, since I'm the kind of person who loves to thumb his nose at authority—and authority figures—it's led me to some interesting situations with a few particularly unsavory bosses. All of those frustrations culminate here in a put-upon protagonist who finds himself working for a horrible corporation run by bosses who are truly too bizarre for words. That was the inspiration, at least. The rest is just my imagination run amok. The sub-title, which I normally don't use, is an homage to a humorous book from the 1950s that was later turned into a musical, *How to Succeed in Business Without Really Trying*. Admittedly I've never read or seen either, but it kept popping into my head while I was writing this story. It seems to fit the surreal nature of the circumstances, which are otherwise pretty bleak, and it makes me giggle, so it stayed.

SHOW ME WHERE IT HURTS

I've only recently begun dabbling in poetry, but I've been a fan of it as long as I can remember. I love song lyrics, jingles, limericks, the filthy rhymes that truckers scrawl on restroom walls. So, this one started out as an exorcism of sorts, of pieces of me that I disliked and wanted to rid from my personality. But then it morphed into something completely different, which is always part of the fun. Anyway, I'd only planned for the poem to have one antagonist, the understood "you" the narrator appears to be complaining about when the poem starts. By the time I got to the end, another antagonist was waiting there in the shadows, someone—or something—dark, dangerous, and hungry. Shout out to some fellow poets who allowed me to run this poem past them without bursting out into laughter, at least not to my face anyway. Appreciate the help, John Baltisberger, Darren Lipman and Benjamin Jones. May the beat always be under your feet.

WE'RE ALL TRAPPED IN AN ETERNALLY RESPAWNING REALITY SITUATION

There's this quarterly writing challenge called *The First Line*. The publisher provides the opening line of your story, and then the writer comes up with the rest. You're not limited to genres and its fun seeing how different writers approach the challenge. The line provided was Jayce recognized the man right away but couldn't remember his name. With most of my stories, I have a good idea where things are going when I begin. With this one, I had no idea. I sat with the prompt for a while, and slowly the opening scene began to emerge. An office worker sees an employee he knows he knows and becomes increasingly bothered when he can't make the connection. Happens to us all sometimes, right? But it really bothers poor Jayce, signaling the beginning of the end. I'm proud that my story was one of six chosen for the issue out of 350 or so entries. Also, I have to admit I had quite a good time putting the screws to my protagonist. Sometimes, writing is like therapy. This is a story that probably has roots in my mother's dementia diagnosis, where she began to slowly forget all the details that made her...well, her. What Jayce is going through isn't dementia, though. His affliction is more existential in nature. The title comes from a joke I cracked at work, in which I lovingly compared office life to existence inside *The Matrix*. It seemed to fit Jayce's psychological conundrum, so it stuck.

CICATRIX

I enjoy experimental fiction, especially stream of consciousness. If you're unfamiliar with this format, it's a type of freeform writing that's usually done in one sitting and is not always beholden to the normal rules of fiction, like structure, grammar and even punctuation. I'd recently read "Undone" by the superb collection *Spontaneous Human Combustion* by Richard Thomas, an author whom I've studied under and whose work I admire. This story began as writing practice on a fine day in fall, where I tried to emulate what Richard did in his tale. For inspiration, I'd found a handful of bizarre photos on the web created by various digital illustrators, and I was shuffling through them trying to find a spark. One image in particular stood out of a deformed young girl in a torn-up black dress standing in a broken down yard. What struck me about the photo was how happy the girl was portrayed. Even though she was obviously born into poverty (the yard, the dress) and had the body of a circus freak, she was smiling the biggest smile into the camera, revealing a mouthful of gleaming, jagged teeth. The ghoul who lives inside my head was, of course, instantly smitten. So, I took a few hours to tell her story. I feel like the stream of consciousness format fits here, because it made sense to me that not only is this girl deformed, but maybe her brain—and thinking processes—are too. I'm disappointed this one never got picked up for publication after a couple of years in circulation, although several publishers wrote back and tell me it was a fine story, just not right for them specifically. So I'm including it here. I'll always love my little Cicatrix.

SPINELESS

One thing you could say about Lloyd on his weekly bar visits: he loved his dogs. He was a genteel kind of guy, a retiree in his early 70s. Kinda quiet. Pour a couple of Glenlivets in him, though, and those dogs were all he talked about. He had two schnauzers, black-haired sisters named Betty and Veronica. "His gals," he called them. They lived with him in his luxury apartment. The gals got their daily walks in front of massive homes on sprawling lots with perfectly manicured lawns. He used to visit me when I was tending bar to tell me how the dogs spent hours at training so they could learn commands like "sit" and "heel". How they cuddled in bed with him at night. How they got the finest dog food he could find. There wasn't much to not like about Lloyd. He was kind, respectful and tipped well. Physically, he was plump, with a rump that drooped over the bar stool. He ate what he wanted and drank what he wanted and exercise be damned. You got the feeling Lloyd was sitting pretty in life, enjoying his retirement to the max. Then he didn't come in for a whole week. Or the next. Or the one after.

One of his friends visited me at the bar a few days later. He told me Lloyd had died of a heart attack alone in his apartment. None of his friends had been expecting him anywhere, so nobody realized he was missing. The apartment manager got suspicious when she noticed a smell. When she finally unlocked the door, she found Lloyd alone. Well, mostly alone. His gals had been cooped up with him. After a few days without food, those schnauzers had to eat something. They'd gone for the softest parts. The pieces of him that were easiest to nibble on. Let's just say the funeral was closed casket.

All these years later, I can't quit thinking about what happened to Lloyd. It was one of those wild, horrible things you just can't predict. The heart attack. The dogs. Their hunger.

HUNGRY

One mild winter day in Dallas, me and the man who would one day become my husband were driving around when I saw this dead guy out in the middle of a parking lot. We pulled over to see what was going on—and that's when the dead guy started moving. He got up, took a few steps across the lot, fell down again, rolled around a few times, and got up again. Obviously, he wasn't dead, he'd only appeared that way for a moment. He was either drunk, high or mentally ill. This went on for several minutes while. We started to call 911 but didn't—he didn't seem to be in danger or a threat to anyone—so we left him there. He never left my mind, though. This is where this story started for me, with Will encountering him in the opening of the story. "Hungry" was a big win, because it was my first story published in an actual book, which was something I'd dreamed about since I was a child.

LOVING THE BEAST

Growing up in Texarkana, Texas, I lived with an unholy fear of the legendary Bigfoot. You see, Texarkana is about 30 miles from Fouke, Arkansas, the home of the legendary Fouke Monster, which was immortalized, at least on a local level, in a low budget film, *The Legend of Boggy Creek.* The Fouke Monster is what the locals call Bigfoot. Like six degrees of Kevin Bacon, everyone I knew back then had a Bigfoot story: Either their cousin had seent it, or their Uncle Jimmy had seent it, or maybe his girlfriend's daddy had seent it when he was out fishin'. Whatever the case, you couldn't go outside at night when I was a kid without the fear of running into the big hairy galoot in the wild. To this drama, I added a story my husband told me of his scariest experience from childhood, of a night when he was alone in his parents' house and heard someone breathing outside his window, *hnhr hnhr hnhr.* It's such a creepy story I had to pay it tribute. The darkness, man. You never know what's out there watching you.

FAMILY TIME

My mother and I were extremely close, so it was especially painful watching her grow old. When she developed dementia during her last years, I wasn't prepared for the toll it would take on our family. It's a horrible disease, one I wouldn't wish on anyone, where your loved one's mind, and eventually, their body, physically change, twist, distort, until you're left with a shell of the person who existed before. When Mom was unable to care for herself at home, we moved her into an assisted living facility with memory care where she could get more help with her dailies. I spent the night with her many times in that facility and I got to see firsthand how some of these patients struggled with their diseases. Sometimes the things they did were laugh-out-loud funny; it would surprise you how impulsive and childlike they could become. Often, they would do things that were downright eerie, almost like they were receiving signals from some unseen, alien force. While Nana in the story isn't my mom, the experience of spending the night in the nursing home with her did happen. I can't tell you how many nights I lay awake in that room with her, listening to old people shrieking out in the darkness, calling for deceased loved ones, or having tantrums, or sobbing for their nurses, while I lay there wide awake, my pulse racing, my mind wandering, wandering...

TREATS

Every trick-or-treater knows the apple story. It was stamped into my head as a kid and is probably still out there circulating to this day. Everyone knows to inspect your candy before eating, because there are some bad grown-ups out there, sweetie, who want to kill you by putting deadly stuff in your candy: razor blades, glass, poison. I remember wondering why anyone would do that. I guess older me is still wondering. So, since fiction writers work out questions just like this on the page, I made it the basis of a story. Why *would* someone do something so horrible to an innocent, unsuspecting child? I came up with sweet Bernice Johnson, who loves Halloween with her whole heart, kinda like I do. Until the night she meets an evil entity who scares her so bad, something in her snaps. It's the only explanation I could come up with, and it doesn't fully explain the evil. Because the short answer is some people are just born rotten, possessed of a hostile urge to hurt, maim, and kill. And really, there's nothing in the world anyone can do about it. Nothing's scarier than people.

THE LAST NIGHT AT THE BLACK BOAR TAVERN

In one of my past lives, professionally speaking, I worked as a bartender. I did it for well over a decade before I retired my church key to write full-time. Once I started honing my writing chops, I knew I wanted to make a bar the setting for a spooky story. Was I successful? I'm not sure the story is truly scary, although it's definitely macabre. It was fun to write, though. I drew inspiration from some of the characters I met along the way in that universe, and the Black Boar Tavern itself is an amalgamation of different places I'd worked over the years. It's fascinating how service culture is its own thing: it has its own language, its own social norms, its own and heroes and villains. The protagonist is someone who is a lot like I was back then. A bit lost in life, unsure of what he wants, looking for a purpose to spin him in a different direction. Not to say all bartenders are that way, but this one certainly was. The protagonist in the story finds his calling, just like I found mine. Although I went a different route than Peter, there's bit of me in these pages, and it felt good to revisit those bars, the people, that world, for a while, at least, in my head. Cheers, loves.

ACKNOWLEDGMENTS

The author would like to thank these sources for publishing the following works for the first time. "The Weeds and the Wildness Yet" was originally published in *Tales from the Lake Vol. V* (Crystal Lake Publishing) in 2019 and is reprinted with permission of the author. "Ghosts on Drugs" was originally recorded as a podcast on *The No Sleep Podcast* in 2020 and is printed with permission of the author. "Mumbo Jumbo" was originally published on the *Grievous Angel* webzine in 2015 and is reprinted with permission of the author. "In the Night, a Whisper" was originally published in *October Screams: A Halloween Anthology* (Kangas Kahn Publishing) in 2023 and is reprinted with permission of the author. "Evil Inc. (or How to Succeed in Business without Really Dying)" was originally published in *The Dead Inside* (Dark Dispatch) in 2022 and is reprinted with permission of the author. "Hungry Waters" was originally published in *Flame Tree Press Newsletter* (Flame Tree) in 2024 and is reprinted with permission of the author. "Gotcha" was originally published in *Max Blood's Mausoleum Vol. 1* (Max Blood Publishing) in 2023 and is reprinted with permission of the author. "We're All Trapped in an Eternally Respawning Reality Situation" was originally published in *The First Line Vol. 27 Spring* (Blue Cubicle Press, LLC) in 2025 and is reprinted with permission of the author. "A Very Stable Zombie" was originally published in *Story Unlikely Newsletter* in 2024 and is reprinted with permission of the author. "Spineless" was originally published in *Dark Moon Digest #57/58* (PMMP Publishing) in 2022 and is reprinted with permission of the author. "The Trouble with Goblins" was originally published on *Wyldwood Press* webzine in 2022 and is reprinted with permission of the author. "Hungry" was originally published in *Creepy Campfire Quarterly* (EMP Publishing) in

2016 and is reprinted with permission of the author. "Loving the Beast" was originally published in *Roadkill Vol. 8: Texas Horror by Texas Authors* (Hell Bound Books Publishing) in 2023 and is reprinted with permission of the author. "When the Nightmare Ends" was originally published on *Dark Recesses* webzine (Dark Recesses Press) in 2022 and is reprinted with permission of the author. "Family Time" was originally published on *2228* webzine in 2020 and is reprinted with permission of the author. "Starstruck" was originally published on *The Dread Machine* webzine in 2021 and is reprinted with permission of the author. "Death by Kittens" was originally published in *100 Ways to Die* (Crow's Feet Press) in 2022 and is reprinted with permission of the author. "A Woman's Place" was originally published in *Year Four: Dark Moments and Patreon* (Black Hare Press) in 2023 and is reprinted with permission of the author. "Losing It" was originally published in *The Binge-Watching Cure Vol. II* (Claren Books) in 2019 and is reprinted with permission of the author. "Gifts" was originally published in *Whispers from the Abyss Vol. II* (01 Publishing) in 2016 and is reprinted with permission of the author. "Treats" was originally published in *Rigor Morbid: Lest Ye Become* (Speakeasy/Bronzeville Books) in 2019 and is reprinted with permission of the author. The works that follow are original and appear in this collection for the first time: "Show Me Where It Hurts", "The Toy Village", "In the Clutches of the Writing Gods", "Cicatrix", "The Aftermath", "Castlemaker", "Those Who Were Asleep", "The Last Night at the Black Boar Tavern" and "The Grouch".

Big shout out from the bottom of my bleak, twisted heart to Richard Thomas, not only for taking the time to write my Foreword and for his guidance over the years, but for being a beacon of light in the dark world of literary horror. New writers need heroes like you—thank you. Thank you to Stephen King for paving the way for generations of horror writers to come, and to Stephen Graham Jones, whose modern work in horror literally inspired me to give it a try myself. A world of thanks to Wulf Moon for sharing his valuable knowledge of storytelling in his Super Secrets of Writing courses. Hugs to the other writing groups I interact with on a not-so regular basis, including Erin MacNair and Kathleen Wallace King, who will always hold a special place in my life, no matter how hard we rip each other's stories to shreds. Big hug to Gordon B. White for mentoring me during one delirious winter with the Horror Writers Association and for his feedback on my story, "The Last Night at the Black Boar Tavern." Thanks to Scarlett R. Algee and JournalStone for thinking enough of these stories to give this little collection a chance. And most importantly, to my family who keeps me going, including the memory of my dearly departed mother, who found a way to be my mom but also my greatest friend—I miss you. To my sister, Jeri, who taught me how to read before kindergarten and always encouraged my writing, no matter how weird it got. To my niece, Ginny, who encourages me by thinking I'm a better writer than I actually am. (Please, nobody tell her—I like it this way.) And to my husband Jim, for the many years of love and support, for grounding me back in reality after I venture into the darkness to wrestle these stories out of the ether, for always believing in me, even on the days when I don't believe in myself. Thank you, sweetie, thank you.

ABOUT THE AUTHOR

Unbeknownst to **ROBERT STAHL**, his body is an empty shell, telepathically controlled by a brain in a jar which was buried long ago under the floorboard of his home. Consequently, his days are filled with the urge to write—stories, letters, articles, whatever. At night he listens to music and when he drifts off to sleep, the brain laughs, a humorless, pitiful sound, as it jiggles alone in the dusty darkness. You can find him on all the socials or on his writing blog, robertestahl.com. He lives in Dallas with his husband and a menagerie of rescue pets. If you enjoyed the book, he'd love a review on Amazon or Goodreads. It really helps!